WOMAN IN THE MIRROR

VOWS FROM THE BEYOND

BOOK EIGHT OF THE *KASTEEL VREDERIC* SERIES

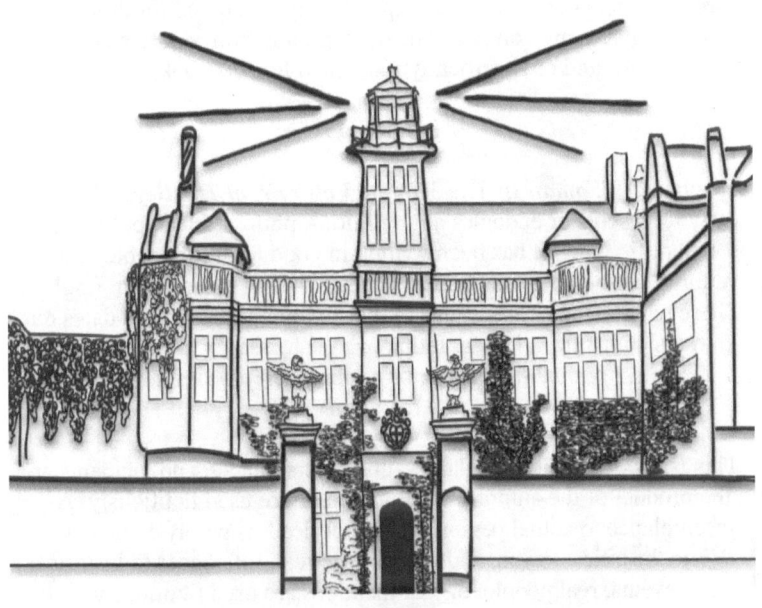

*"Even beyond death, I will
watch you like a star from the skies. Or as a
butterfly, I will be with you on Earth. Yet forever, I
will be by you as the woman in the mirror."*

Ann Marie Ruby

Disclaimer:

This book ("*Woman In The Mirror: Vows From The Beyond*") in no
way represents or endorses any religious, philosophical, political, or
scientific view. It has been written in good faith for people of all
cultures and beliefs. This book has been written in American English.
There may be minor variations in the spelling of names and dates due
to translations from Dutch, Indian, English, and Egyptian provincial
dialects, regional languages, or minor discrepancies in historical
records.

This is a work of fiction. Names, characters, places, and incidents are
the product of the author's imagination or are used fictitiously. Any
resemblance to actual persons, living or dead, is purely coincidental.
While the cities, towns, and villages are real, references to historical
events, real people, or real locations are used fictitiously.

Published in the United States of America, 2024.

ISBN-13: 979-8-9917416-2-0

DEDICATION

"Love never dies as love reincarnates with the beholders as they search for one another, life after life, keeping themselves alive through love."

I dedicate this book to my beloved furry baby boy, Mr. Patches Ruby (2009-2024), a Shih Tzu dog. He passed away during the publication of this book. He had loved me all his life and now all my life, I will keep his memories alive by loving him and all furry animals. Love never dies and through love, the beholders of this love also are eternal.

In this book, I tell you the immortal story of a couple who had through their love crossed time and place. They proved love never dies. Through eternal endless love, they made their love story historical, epical, and immortal.

Today if you are questioning your Creator how He could separate twin flames and their journey, or separate a family member from another family member, or a friend from you, remember you are not separated just because you don't see one another. Ask yourself if you can see, smell, or hear love that pulls you toward your beloved. You can't, yet you do feel the love, the separation, the joys, and the pains of this journey. Then, believe in your love and know your story is never over or complete as long as you two keep on remembering one another.

Believe in yourself and your beloved. Believe in reincarnation as it will give you another chance in another life. You must keep believing in another life and another time, you will unite. Until then, keep writing your stories through memories. Live, laugh, and love life until you awaken in another life and in another time when you will meet again.

To all pet parents, I give you my blessings for adopting a pet even though you know they have a short lifespan. As life is only a day, enjoy this day to the fullest. Give and share this human love with all our animal friends and let's in union make this world a safer and healthier home for all.

The hardest part of writing this book was losing my furry boy, Patches. Every time I wrote something, he would sit not next to my feet but on my feet. He wanted to know I was there, and he always napped on my feet. The funny part is I had to always make sure not to jump up while he was there.

Tears were my only friend while I finished this book for him in his memory. Before I finished this book, however, I adopted Moo Patches Ruby, a Shih Tzu who looks so similar to Patches as all Shih Tzus do, yet very different. I consider him to be Patches's younger brother. In my dream, I saw Patches had sent Moo to me, so I would have his brother with me. Moo too has taken up the same spot as he sits on my feet when I am writing anything. This furry boy came and even though I call him Moo, he is actually my healer. With his love, Moo healed my broken heart.

Dear Patches, I know you have traveled through the tunnel of light and will awaken as a human boy. Your eternal soul will travel like a bird and find your beloved family members. May you find a kind and loving family like your kind and loving soul. My love for you will be there with you in all your reincarnated lives.

In honor of my beloved dog who lived to be almost sixteen years old, here is a poem I had written for my beloved furry boy, Mr. Patches Ruby.

IMMORTALIZED

Loved you

My beloved Patches,

From the first bark

To the last bark!

From your first breath to

Your last breath!

Loved you from dawn

Till dusk through dawn.

My dear boy,

You gave me your

Whole life to enjoy you,

To love you,

To be with you!

Yet now,

Throughout my whole life,

I will miss you.

I will remember you.

I will never stop

Loving you.

I know

As you gave me

Joy your whole life,

I will give back this joy

To all of your

Brothers,

Sisters, and

Your furry friends

As they love us

Throughout their entire lives,

And we the

Human families will

Love, cherish, and

Remember all of our

Furry families

Eternally.

For you my beloved Patches,

I will eternally

Keep on

Loving you

For the rest of

My life,

As you loved me

Throughout your

Entire existence.

My love has now become immortal

As it made a furry family

And a human family

Bond eternally

Through

Our unconditional love.

For you,

My beloved Patches,

I will always

Immortalize

Our journey.

Your journey has ended,

But as I continue,

I will remember,

Our journey together

Through love

Is now and forever

IMMORTALIZED.

TABLE OF CONTENTS

PROLOGUE:

HAZY LONDON

"Forever framed
Inside a frame,
We see you
Only gaze at us,
Yet we are united
Through our eyes,
Oh,
Woman in the mirror."

London's cool winter brought cloudy skies and light precipitation around the city as we landed at Heathrow Airport. I decided to take a short detour in London before joining my family members in Naarden, the Netherlands to continue with our journey to Egypt.

The thought of what laid ahead of me sent cold shivering sparks through my entire body. My wife, Dr. Margriete van Phillip, accompanied me as we had left our daughter with Mama and Papa.

Margriete tugged on my hand as she said, "Jacobus, you're shivering! Your hands feel cold. I can hear your teeth chattering. Are you all right? This isn't like your character. We've gone through so much more! It's all going to be all right."

I simply admire my beloved gorgeous wife who has so much confidence in her. I am extremely grateful to be with her in situations that I dread. All the people on this Earth think I, Dr. Jacobus Vrederic van Phillip, am filled with all the confidence on this Earth. It's my mother Anadhi Newhouse van Phillip who gifts me with all the needed confidence and hope.

I stood there silent as I was still observing Margriete with love. She had insisted on coming along with me on this trip. Memories of everything we went through together had brought a sudden burst of warm comfort to my chest.

Margriete understood my thoughts as she said, "Evermore beloved, I have reincarnated only to be with you. Not just to be together in one life, but in all my incarnations and beyond. I'm here with you. We will get over all the obstacles somehow, someway."

I held my wife and walked into a lab that held the hidden mystery we had been waiting for. The building looked like a hospital where people were being treated. It didn't have any deadly diseases but just regular checkups and lab reports.

Within this building, hidden in plain sight was a research center where the world's top scientists were all busy trying to find the next biggest cure for this world. This hospital was completely funded and built through my father's blessings. It's named after my ancestors as we call it the Vrederic Hospital London. My family had been involved in various scientific research included lifesaving drugs and immortality serums.

Everyone was wearing hazmat suits covering all parts of their bodies so that nothing was exposed. At times, it felt like we were walking in a sci-fi thriller. Margriete and

I walked into a lab where we met our acquaintance, Dr. Hans Avyaan, a Dutch Indian scientist.

He seemed very excited to see us, yet somehow, I felt he was different. My whole interior felt the chills again as if my sixth sense was warning me there was something more to this man. Why did I get the chills seeing a scientist who was helping us?

He gestured us to follow him to another room and he led us through an underground glass tunnel which had fish swimming above and beyond it. We walked without talking for fifteen minutes before we found ourselves in a room. There was a door that looked like a stone wall, but it opened and let us out. We entered a courtyard, surrounded by waterfalls and colorful birds sitting on trees. It was like we just entered a magical place hidden somewhere either beneath or above the grounds.

In the courtyard, there were a lot of sarcophagi hidden inside other boxes that were older than time, or they were brought here from the pyramids of Giza. I realized this is where scientists had brought the box containing the sarcophagus of my uncle, Kees van Vrederic, inside. Dr. Avyaan was the same scientist who had sent a living and walking man found in a sarcophagus back to our home, the famous Kasteel Vrederic in Naarden.

Dr. Avyaan broke the silence as he said, "Kees is the only person who walked out from a sarcophagus, even though your family members have denied this fact. I really need to warn you. Kees must take things a little slowly because the sunlight will affect him. Somewhat like vampires, but reverse. He needs to be in the sun and even at night, he needs light to stay alive. He still isn't completely safe in his human body."

Dr. Avyaan was thinking about what he would share with us and what he wouldn't share as he became quiet. He rubbed his dark black hair and closed his blue eyes for a few seconds. He was fair-skinned and looked Dutch but had his Indian mother's features in him.

Like him, I too have a mix of Dutch, Indian, and American genes. I wondered why he never spoke about his personal life. I didn't even know if he was married or had a family. Never do I pry on anyone's personal lives as my family members never decide who to hire but a board does.

Dr. Avyaan whispered with a very frightening voice, "Strangely in another coffin, we found some blood and fingerprints, but no body. I believe we only were able to recover half of the coffin. The scientists in Egypt said they recovered some parts of the coffin and kept all of it safe for you. They found some clothes and jewelry there. The scientists are still excavating the findings. In the meantime, we were able to get two fingerprints from the coffin. One set of fingerprints belongs to Marinda van Vrederic, your aunt, but we don't have any evidence as you gave us shadows of fingerprints."

My knees felt like they were giving up on me. I held myself up as I did thousands of times for my patients. I got inside of my doctor's body and drew out all my confidence. My eyes kept going to all the mirrors Dr. Avyaan had around the place.

I asked him, "You only found blood stains and fingerprints that matched the prints and blood we had provided to you, yet no body. So, you're saying in Egypt, there are no bodies but just fingerprints and some personal belongings? Am I correct?"

Margriete started to walk back and forth while still observing both of us. She kept touching weird mirrors and I assumed she was thrilled by all the antique mirrors. Personally, mirrors scare me unless my wife is on them. For the first time since we arrived and had been with Dr. Avyaan, Margriete spoke.

She questioned him directly, "What about the fingerprints I had sent you? Those were prints of a demon who had lived centuries ago. I had said the prints which we were able to recover from Malibu, California are of extreme urgency. We must get the results back."

There was pin-drop silence in the room again until Dr. Avyaan said, "It's strange as those fingerprints match an eighteen-year-old teenage woman who has been hunting down young men and women here in England for the past two years. She has been linked to all of these crimes as her fingerprints match the murderer of a lot of young people, all virgins. She even admitted to all her crimes. Because there is no evidence of her ever being physically at any of the crime scenes, she was arrested and released every time. She shrieks and laughs when she gets released. The authorities think she is just a crazy woman trying to be famous and wants to be the infamous killer."

He walked over to a bird who was trying to fly, but I saw she had a broken wing. I stood in awe witnessing our famous human doctor somehow heal the bird with his hands and let her rest in a cage. I realized all these birds and the underground sea creatures were being treated by this strange magical doctor. This was a magical healing place for animals, and I presumed humans and animals both get the same treatment from him.

Dr. Avyaan smiled at the bird and continued, "The teenager has never physically left England. She, however, claims she leaves in her sleep and murders people or does really bad things to them. The girl said she isn't frightened by the crimes she has committed and never felt bad. Rather, she is thrilled that no one living or dead could ever link her to these crimes."

Dr. Avyaan was clearly still thinking silently as he treated his wounded birds. There were so many just waiting for him patiently. He then started to talk out loud, as if he never stopped and never lost his train of thought.

The doctor very calmly said, "She has been living with a lot of people in a small village who will testify she never set her feet outside of England. Her fingerprints are found with all the murder victims all over the world. Yes, they match the fingerprints you sent over. Your fingerprints match one woman who had lived centuries ago named Succubus. The teenager who never left the small village is also known as Succubus, although some call her Alice. The weird part is they both have the same fingerprints which is scientifically not possible."

Dr. Avyaan inspected Margriete very closely with his eyes. My confident wife did not move, nor did she shrug away. She held my hands in hers, signaling to me she did not like the man's stares.

He said, "Your face is so familiar to a sketch I'm trying to do. Somehow, I drew a woman in my sketchbook with wavy brown hair in a bun, like the women centuries ago used to place their hair in. My model didn't have olive skin or raven black hair. She was the European version of the Snow White character. You, however, are hmm…the Indian version. I'm a collector of old arts, especially sketches. I promise your face seems so familiar as if your face was in a sketch I have seen somewhere."

In the room, there were so many sketches of various people, but all were on mirrors. It felt strange and somehow scary. There were mirrors without any sketches and instead of feeling it was normal, I felt like something was missing and some sketches of more people would just appear. In my mind, I kept seeing my wife's face on a mirror, but I couldn't figure out where I had seen it. Even though it was brain scratching, I had a weird feeling I shouldn't think about where I had seen her face and should just wipe the thought out of my mind.

Margriete, a doctor herself, watched Dr. Avyaan take care of the birds. She then asked me, "Jacobus, how is this possible? Are we saying Succubus is living through a teenager or has reincarnated, or what? How could a dead woman from centuries ago have the same fingerprints as a teenager today who has confessed to committing murders?"

Dr. Avyaan sat down on a bench near his birds and said, "All the activities surrounding this teenage woman named Succubus or Alice or whatever she calls herself, are highly suspicious. No one knows when or where she was born. Authorities are trying to find out where she came from or to which nation she belongs. To me it seems like she might have just popped out of a mirror and will go back in it as soon as her work is done."

Margriete and I locked our eyes onto one another. We knew something was not adding up, but we didn't say anything. My wife and I realized our brains had to go into a no-thinking-anything mode so that no one could telepathically take our thoughts.

Dr. Avyaan laughed out loud, and this time quietly whispered, "As a doctor, I know she is only eighteen years old. It's strange how some crimes linking to her are centuries old. She has no birth history as if she somehow travels time, finds a human body, and then just becomes a real living and breathing human. It's somewhat like Kees. Marinda, however, is different as we couldn't find any scientific proof of her ever dying, just her fingerprints and her blood. I couldn't share this with anyone. Even the scientific society has a limit as to what they will believe and what they will discard. If these theories were to ever get leaked, the world would go into a panic mode, and we would have on our hands a scientific and societal catastrophe."

I wanted to inquire much more from him, yet I didn't know where to begin. As a doctor myself, I knew he was an Earthly man who too had his limits. Margriete who never hid her thoughts, however, had a theory.

She said out loud, "So Succubus has somehow taken a human form. She tried to kill Uncle Kees and I believe Aunt Marinda, but she failed as true love saved both. Now we must find Aunt Marinda or her body. It seems like the answers to our questions are buried in Egypt. Jacobus, we must be ready if her body isn't over there. That's not so bad. We'll do whatever we must to protect our family members, all of them."

Dr. Avyaan again glared at Margriete for a while, and he then brought out a file from underneath a bird cage. He gave the file to me and gestured to open the very heavy folder he placed in my hands. The folder had on top of it in all caps, TOP SECURTY. I opened the folder and found inside were pictures of Succubus we had seen in Malibu.

In clear words, there was a note which read,

"A dead woman from centuries ago lives. Numerous research papers prove all the blood works and fingerprints match crimes that were being committed centuries ago. All unsolved mysteries from different centuries had the same set of fingerprints. How could one woman who lives in a small village near London, who has never left her village or home, have the identical fingerprints to the one who was known to be a demoness?

The crimes are much older than the predator. How this is even possible, we can't prove with any scientific evidence. So, we will close this file until something comes up as evidence or as a hoax."

These were paranormal activities which is why there were no answers for the human minds. Yet my family members are not just humans. We are the immortal family members of the paranormal Kasteel Vrederic. I knew Margriete and I had to travel back home to Naarden so that with my whole family, we could investigate another thriller that awaits to be solved.

I told both, "I believe Succubus was reborn. She has the fingerprints of a human body which proves reincarnation even more. How else would a dead and a living person have the same fingerprints? She is using the tunnel of dreams to travel and commit these crimes. We'll prove it even if that's the last thing we do. If she was reborn, then how did she keep her demoness powers? I'm guessing she is traveling time."

We were all lost in our own thoughts. I knew we had to go to Egypt but only worried if we had to go somewhere else. I was unsure if our friend Dr. Avyaan was smirking or laughing. Maybe he was just an awkward person who didn't know how to express his feelings.

He said, "I would like you to know, your family members are being investigated. News that a family member of yours might be a vampire has been selling like hotcakes within the high security agencies. This news has made your family members top suspects. Another rumor sprawling in the air is that your family members don't age. Either way, all of you try to stay low and let these rumors subside."

Margriete just laughed and looked to me for a response. I knew she wanted support from me to say something to defend my family members. I kept my thoughts to myself and said nothing as Dr. Avyaan smiled and tried to avoid any further discussion related to this topic.

He said, "I told them then all the people who have had plastic surgeries or take good care of themselves must all be vampires. I also told them maybe you are time

14

travelers and have a woman with a mirror who assists you in time traveling."

I said nothing as I told my wife through our twin flame telepathy to not say anything. I told her mind-to-mind, don't bring attention to us but take it away from us. Also, I didn't know how much I trusted this Dr. Avyaan who I presumed was our friend but might just be the enemy trying to place all the fault upon our shoulders. For some weird reason, he seemed to be fixated on a mirror with Margriete's sketched face.

I told our friend or foe, "You guys gave us an empty sarcophagus. A sarcophagus we had not asked for but were given as you all presumed it belonged to us. You can't link my family to anything as the sarcophagus was your own experiment, not ours. My family members have helped, only at your request, with our scientific and psychic abilities. Neither do we know any sarcophagus nor were we ever shown proof of any sarcophagus."

Our doctor friend or foe winked at us and agreed to not talk about this anymore. I knew Uncle Kees's name would be brought up throughout all these investigations as there was no proof of him being born in the last century. My only hope was no one had any proof we were ever given any sarcophagus. If they say they did, then they would have to testify why they had given a family a sarcophagus in the first place.

Before we headed out, Dr. Avyaan reminded us again, "Jacobus if you or Margriete ever do get your hands on a mirror that has a sketch of Margriete, keep it safe and don't talk to anyone about it."

I thought to myself if I did have one, I wouldn't share it with anyone anyway, especially not with a person who deals with sarcophagi and antique mirrors. For some reason in the corner of my mind, I saw a sketch of Margriete gazing at me. I looked back and forth for one second as I thought I was hearing Dr. Avyaan scratching his fingers on mirrors like he was trying to open a door within them. Margriete had the same vision and jumped closer to me.

Dr. Avyaan's obsession with mirrors seemed peculiar. Why would the famous scientist who experiments with sarcophagi and deadly diseases be surrounded by a collection of antique mirrors? The thought bothered me a lot. I wanted to ask him but thinking of Aunt Marinda, Uncle Kees, and the mystery of the woman in the mirror prevented me from uttering any more words.

This is the love story of my Uncle Kees, the only surviving member of my family who still carries the original Van Vrederic surname as he was interred in a sarcophagus centuries ago. He had awakened to find out the love of his life and my beloved Aunt Marinda, the time traveler, had been imprisoned in a mirror. She can travel through time as she had been a time traveler but now is getting weak and might not make it and disappear eternally.

A love story that had begun centuries ago now awaits to be completed through the magical tree of life, as we the descendants of the Van Vrederic family must unite these eternal lovers. They had been protecting the magical Kasteel Vrederic family members throughout time. When and where we needed help, we were given help through the blessed hands of Aunt Marinda, a time-traveling psychic. Aunt Marinda and her twin flame Uncle Kees's love story that begun must come to an end through the union of the separated lovers who await to be united through life and or death as love never dies, even in death.

The secret Margriete and I had brought with us was buried within our chest. We didn't share with anyone, but I worried why Dr. Avyaan kept on asking about a third mirror we didn't have. We had the two mirrors. The first mirror was a medallion which had a mirror inside of it with Succubus the demoness imprisoned within it. The second mirror had Aunt Marinda imprisoned by Succubus in it. Both mirrors were brought back from Malibu to Naarden with us and both had their pictures on them.

Today, however, both of the mirrors had neither Succubus nor Aunt Marinda's pictures in them. It was as if both walked out, or Succubus had something to do with it. So, we assumed Succubus escaped somehow and either took Aunt Marinda with her or I hoped beyond hope that Aunt Marinda had escaped from Succubus the demoness. Either way, we would need to find Aunt Marinda and solve the mystery of who the woman in the mirror is, and why as soon as possible. Also, I have to figure out the mystery of the third mirror.

Margriete was shaking in fear as we walked out from Dr. Avyaan's quarters. She said, "Jacobus, I don't want to ever be imprisoned in a mirror. I'm scared, what was that man hinting at? Am I going to be dead and imprisoned in a mirror?"

I held on to my wife tightly and tried to comfort her. I didn't want her to know I too was frozen cold at the same thought. Whatever it may take, I would not allow my wife to travel alone.

I heard my phone ringing, startling Margriete and me. Margriete answered the phone, and it was the children calling.

Theunis Peters, our young boy soldier asked, "Margriete, you are okay? You were calling me, I heard you. Remember, never fear okay because I am here. Love you Margriete, you too Jacobus. Come to us safely, okay?"

Margriete hung up the phone after telling them how much she missed all of them. Margriete's tears began rolling out of her eyes as she found her peace of mind. I realized these were tears of comfort, not tears of grief or terror.

I am Jacobus Vrederic van Phillip, the original diarist of the Kasteel Vrederic diaries. Now as a doctor and a scientific scholar, I must solve this mystery which has haunted my family members for centuries. I have named this diary *Woman In The Mirror* as that's the only clue we have of where Aunt Marinda is. Now, in this diary we have a mystery of three mirrors. Two of which we know but the third one is a mystery.

Dear Aunt Marinda, guide us to where you are, maybe through our dreams or through the magical walls of Kasteel Vrederic. As we go home with hope, we will be guided to you, so that we can unite Uncle Kees and you in ever after. Be it on Earth or beyond, true love stories should never be cut short nor should twin flames trying to create another immortal love story ever be separated. I will find you and somehow unite the twin flames that started to write the original love story of Kasteel Vrederic. The lost son who still to this day caries the surname Van Vrederic has awakened and asks why then his beloved has not awakened.

He had been waiting for his beloved for centuries. He said to me personally that his beloved has been guiding and protecting the Kasteel Vrederic family members for centuries. Now Uncle Kees has asked me to help and somehow unite one of the original twin flames of Kasteel Vrederic somehow, someway.

I give you both my personal oath. I will try to do this dead or alive for I am your beloved nephew, Jacobus Vrederic van Phillip, checking out from hazy London.

HAZY LONDON

I wonder

If mirrors could talk

Or if they could react

Without we the people

In front of them,

Asking or saying anything.

What about the pictures

Of our past?

Could they awaken

And talk to us?

Could they maybe inform us

Where they had gone

After their bodies

Had departed this world?

When we go

On a journey,

Our beloved families

Await our calls,

To let them know

We have arrived

At our destination

Safely.

I ask you the departed,

Give us a call.
Let us know
Your journey
Had taken you safely
To your destination.
For us,
You are now a painting
Hanging on the walls,
Yet I know this world
Is a mirror.
When you the
Departed souls leave,
You can see us
Even though
We can't see you.
You then become
Like a shadow
On the dark walls.
You watch us
Like the glowing stars.
We are lost
And confused
Evermore.
Where and how

Do we find you

When your body

Is nowhere

To be found?

Everything became

Even more blurred

As we arrived

In

HAZY LONDON.

CHAPTER ONE:

EGYPT, LAND OF THE PYRAMIDS

"Predators fear their
Victims might awaken
And solve the unsolved
Murder mysteries.
At the door of miracles,
The predators and their
Victims meet again as
This is when the dead
Tell their side
Of the story and
Capture the predators."

The Sahara Desert at night was very cold. The temperature dropped rapidly as it does in the deserts. The temperature variations from day to night were huge. At night, the temperature was -4°C (25°F), however, during the day it was 38°C (100°F).

My father, the best pilot ever on this world in our eyes, had flown us to Egypt on his own plane. It is easier that way as with his contacts we can be at places normally people are not allowed to be at. My family and I were able to watch the popular sound and light show that illuminates the pyramids of Giza. During this show, we heard the history behind how an ancient civilization had built these miraculous structures.

Egypt, the land of mystery, brings travelers from around the globe to its mystical land. Some travel in hope of finding lost treasures. Some flock to this place searching for the lost ancient mysteries. This land, surrounded by ancient and modern-day architectures, is a mystery beyond human detection. There are around 118 ancient masonry structures in Egypt that are called pyramids. My family and I wanted to visit a special pyramid far away from the famous pyramids which are the burial grounds of ancient pharaohs.

The Sahara Desert touches eleven countries. We were going to cross the desert to some of these eleven countries in search of one special pyramid. This was a pyramid no one knew about, yet we were advised by Dr. Avyaan to the pyramid Uncle Kees was buried within. This pyramid had some personal belongings of Aunt Marinda and her fingerprints. Maybe she was there or maybe somehow, we could get something that would inform us where she was.

My mother, a famous dream psychic, always knows a lot more than she shares. She wants the facts and science to back up her dreams before she follows any of them. For a while, Mama was deep in her thoughts. Her eyes seemed worried.

She asked Papa, "Erasmus, did you get special permission from your friends or the government? We need to cross the borders and see where our trail leads. Can we sleep in the pyramids of our choice overnight to investigate our theory? I hear the pyramids have small spaces after their sarcophagus chambers where people still sleep with sleeping bags in the tiny corners."

Mama paused and from her look, I knew something was coming as she said loudly, "Also, Jacobus, Mama needs to use the bathroom and these tombs you all call pyramids have none."

Papa talked to Mama soundlessly as he held her in his embrace and kissed her head. That is Papa's way of not saying what he knows to the whole crowd. I smiled as these two always bring cheer back into my life. No matter how hard the going gets, my mother and father always make things seem better. I said nothing and enjoyed witnessing my parents smile and talk on their own.

A happy couple spreads happiness around their home and to their future generations. My parents hugged their grandchildren and laughed as they kissed the girls and the boys. I treasure this simple, yet very powerful attribute of my parents as do my brothers. Both my brothers, Andries and Antonius, were watching Mama and Papa and felt better. It's like it matters not what we must go through, Mama and Papa are here, so everything is just fine.

Our journey took us to a particular pyramid in Egypt. This mound of Earth was not counted as one of the known pyramids in Egypt. It was a lost site not seen nor heard of by anyone until recently. It's strange how this pyramid was all by itself and nothing could be seen anywhere near it. The place felt unnerving, and I could feel the hair behind my neck rise.

This structure was made just like all the other pyramids were made. It was, however, a newer structure according to the archeologists who guided us to the location. The ancient pyramids were built around 2700 B.C., and some are thought to have been built around 1500 B.C. This one was only a few centuries old and was lost and buried under the great Sahara Desert.

Usually, pyramids are above ground, but this one was buried deep beyond the Earth. This structure wasn't visible to human eyes until recently. It was still unknown to most even though it isn't far from the Great Pyramid of Giza. A group of scientific scholars newly discovered this pyramid, and they found a sarcophagus buried within the pyramid.

My family and I arrived at this structure after Margriete and my trip to London led us to this mysterious place. This journey was very hard as we brought all our family members with us, even the young children. My mother always insists she will travel with everyone.

If something happens and we travel time or get lost in another time zone, she wants to be with all her children and grandchildren. Her reasoning is then no one is left behind to worry about the others. It matters not what the public thinks, but our family lives together, travels together, and stands by one another through life and even beyond death.

I really didn't know if it was a good idea to bring everyone on this trip. My mother had her reasonings and no one wanted to stay behind. My brothers all insisted if one comes, then the others would follow. So, the public with their harsh judgments could see we were on a family vacation. They would not suspect we were on a trip to find the origins of a very fearful sarcophagus and find the missing coffin of our beloved Aunt Marinda.

What Margriete and I didn't share with anyone is the weird mirror Dr. Avyaan had spoken about. I felt strange thinking about my wife being in a mirror. I know some say the souls of the dead can get trapped in a mirror. So, we both decided we wouldn't talk about it unless it became an issue.

No one wanted to bring Succubus's name upon their lips in fear that just by doing so, she would be standing inside the pyramid alive and watching over her prisoners. One lifelong prisoner was with us traveling to the pyramid where he was imprisoned for centuries. In this day and age, people would compare him to a vampire. In my family, however, he is our Uncle Kees even though he is still in his original four-hundred-year-old vehicle.

He is a twin son of the original Van Vrederic sons. The other twin was reincarnated and is my father Erasmus van Phillip. Even though they are brothers from a different life, in my household all births from different time periods have no time limit. Reborn over and over with memories intact from all our births connected all our lifetimes into one storyline.

Today, we are the famous Kasteel Vrederic's immortal family members. Rumors have spread that I miraculously turned my family members young. Let the rumors be, for I shall carry all the burdens of every single member of my family any time, any day.

Uncle Kees was talking with Papa inaudibly as we camped on the sand dunes of the great Sahara Desert. There were no other sightseers or overnight campers on these grounds as all must have special permission to camp here by a tomb, a pyramid, that was just discovered recently. I knew this was the tomb Uncle Kees was buried in. The sarcophagus that used to be at the center of this pyramid was of Uncle Kees.

Uncle Kees gave Papa a diary he had carried with him. The diary looked very old. I knew this was buried with Uncle Kees because he had refused to let it go. In the dark campground where no sounds could be heard, Uncle Kees stood up.

I worried about Aunt Marinda's personal belongings being found in the pyramid. Although Dr. Avyaan had said personal belongings were left here, were they missing because they were with Uncle Kees? I speculated if this was a trap, and they wanted whatever was with Uncle Kees. I froze and wondered if Mama had any clues or had any dreams of us being tricked.

Uncle Kees came to me and said, "In this diary, you will read about my eternal love story. A story that started centuries ago and is still being written as one always remembers the saddest days of our lives, not the happiest. My love story retells the thirst of two lovers who never had a chance in life to live our whole lives together. Our story started with a coffin, the same box we are searching for today that was here in this pyramid where I was buried. Your Aunt Marinda was also in a coffin. I always wondered where she was buried because as far as I can recall, she was never here."

I took the centuries-old diary and sat by my family members. My young daughter Rietje and my niece Griet sat near my wife and me. They were joined by their friends, the two young boys. The father of the lighthouse, Theunis's young and reincarnated self, and the great warrior, Alexander's young and reincarnated self, were brought miraculously to us by Aunt Marinda. My two brothers Andries and Antonius came and sat by me as their wives Tara Bella and Katelijne picked up Rietje and Griet on their laps and sat near Mama, Papa, and Uncle Kees.

The first few pages of the diary read,

"Dear beloved Kees and the family members of my beloved's home Kasteel Vrederic,

I had promised to love and always follow my heart to love and honor my given vows of love. My beloved husband Kees, I will be found as your love for me and my love for you will always keep us in an everlasting bridge that will never collapse. Promises made to be together in life or in death through the bond of love, I have kept.

We will be together. Our love story will be immortal through our immortal love. As stars of the desert's skies or the flowers on a gravesite, I will stay near you eternally. Never leave me alone my beloved as I never left you alone but am with you always.

My beloved, remember to find the secret staircase that is hidden in one of the pyramids in the great Sahara Desert. Yes, the same staircase Succubus uses to be at different places in short periods of time. These pyramids are connected to Saturn and to Mars. In Saturn, be careful as that is where she and her husband Incubus live. It is rumored people use this staircase to travel time.

Yes, it's true. I too have used this staircase to travel time. That's how I could be with all of you even after death or during my imprisonment. I don't know though if you will ever find this staircase. It's hidden within the Earth and the skies. Succubus is from my bloodline, so I was able to travel through this. It sounds weird to even think I am related to her by blood, though it hurts that she is from my bloodline.

I had brought Theunis and Alexander to you through this same staircase. That's how they became children and safe from the capture of the demonic world and the demons. Theunis should always be kept safely. I left him in your care Margriete, as you must at all times keep him safe.

Today, you have the two warriors from Mars with you who are related to them. Theunis is related through birth and Alexander through marriage. I can't say when you will receive this diary. I will keep writing in this diary in hope that sometime in the future, our nephew Jacobus van Vrederic will reincarnate as Jacobus Vrederic van Phillip and find it.

Also, Theunis should have given you a gift Margriete. I hope I remember the gift and remind all of you about it soon. I won't write about it in fear of my diary falling into the wrong hands.

It's Jacobus's destiny to find this diary and help free me from this prison of Succubus. I have been her prisoner for centuries, but I have used her own ways to travel and to save and be with my family members in their times of need. Succubus who had as many men as she wanted had eyed and wanted the only man she could never have, in her dreams or in reality, the only man who I know is my twin flame, my husband, my Kees.

Also do remember the forbidden relationships in this world. Amongst them, one is between an uncle and niece. Kees was married into the family, so he is not related by blood to Succubus. Still, in my eyes, it's forbidden. As we were taught to run away from all things that are forbidden, she runs toward all that is forbidden.

Don't ever forget my dear family, this evil woman has different given names. Succubus is a name for demonesses as Incubus is a name for demons. These demons are born at times in human form, as saints too are born in human form. So, always let your sixth sense judge who is good and who is bad. I pray you don't mistake Succubus for me and me for her as she has been trying to take my form for centuries.

Their kind of people, or demons, are dangerous and come to these deserts to find immortality. They travel through these deserts through hidden staircases in the pyramids to find immortality and power.

The deserts and the pyramids are the only places and structures on Earth that resemble places and structures within the planets above the skies.

That's why the pharaohs had these tombs built like pyramids, so they can travel time and become immortal. I too am a time traveler through these tombs. Find my missing body and I shall travel time to it and unite and awaken from there on.

I don't want immortality but to unite with my beloved eternally. Let our love story be immortal, not our bodies. If you can't find the staircase, and I advise don't try to find the staircase if you don't have to, then you will enter but might not be able to exit. So, wait for someone to come to you who might help. I feel like my body is somewhere near London. I was in a pyramid near Giza, but they keep moving me. I wait for you all to free me from this imprisonment of Succubus."

In front of my eyes, the diary was again blank and there were no other words written in it. It was as if suddenly, everything was erased.

I told my mother, "I am disoriented. What just happened? I saw the diary was fully complete to the end. Everything just vanished like the words were written with magical ink. I don't know what to do. I'm a scientist, a doctor, and I only walk with science. Yet my life only gives me mysteries that science can't agree with or verify."

My two brothers stood up and took the diary from my hands as Andries said, "Cool Big Bro, we get to solve another mystery. I'm excited to begin and don't care about the sex maniac Succubus. We had encountered her before, and we will again deal with her. Tonight, let's celebrate what we do have and not what we don't have."

Mama came over and kissed her baby boy Andries's head as automatically Antonius and I ran over to her.

She kissed both of us too and then said, "Jacobus, I am proud of all three of my boys. We will solve this mystery as a family. We're good immortals fighting with an evil immortal soul. My children must remember always in a war between good and bad, good always wins. We will through tears, sorrows, and laughters, be victorious again. I believe this diary was filled with words because we are sitting under the magical staircase above us. We can't travel through it but will travel through Earth to find Aunt Marinda."

Tears were spilling from everyone's eyes. Our children were napping, and I hoped they missed our storytelling hour. Yet I saw the teardrop that was falling from our girl with the lantern, Griet's eyes. She said nothing but only watched Theunis who was sleeping on Margriete's lap. If eyes could tell a story, these two knew so much more as their past life memories were intact. As warriors and time travelers, they were burdened with so much more and I only wished we could maybe give these children some normalcy.

My mother told me with her eyes not to say anything. I gestured toward her I won't. Yet again a certain mirror's image floated in my head. I saw this time my daughter Rietje and my niece Griet were sitting by the mirror. Like a cloud above the skies, the image just evaporated. I let the thoughts go, as it must be my overactive mind trying to make something out of nothing. The night was getting chilly as Papa and Uncle Kees talked quietly amongst themselves.

I told my family, "Well everyone, let's celebrate tonight. As history often repeats itself, this time we will make sure the predator is the victim not the innocent. For this time, the story is in our hands and on our terms, we will meet her again. Let's be happy and believe at the end of the tunnel there is light, as we have all landed safely in Egypt, the land of pyramids."

EGYPT, THE LAND OF PYRAMIDS

Dawn breaks open

As the sun brings

All memories,

And

All hidden

Secrets

Into the open.

The sand dunes

In the deserts

Hide

Secrets

Of the past,

The present,

And the future,

As invisible staircases

Appear

And disappear.

In the

Secret tombs

Of the past

Mysterious tombs

Where the sarcophagi

Are stored

Are not to

Be disturbed.

It is known

We should

Always leave

The dead

Alone

To be buried

In peace.

Yet the

Mysterious

Door,

The invisible staircase

The dead use

To travel time

And to be

Immortal

Are used,

Not only

By the good,

But by

The evil

Too.

For like the

Sand dunes

Of the deserts,

These staircases

Are hidden and

Found

By the

Third eyes

Of the

Seers,

Which shall

Solve

The mysteries

Hidden

To the humans

On Earth.

The staircases

Everyone

Searches

For

Are hidden

In the

Sahara Desert

Within

One of the eleven

Countries,

In or near

EGYPT, THE LAND OF PYRAMIDS.

CHAPTER TWO:

THE SAHARA DESERT

"The mind must conquer
Its battle against
Any and
All optical illusions
When the physical
And spiritual bodies
Seek the truth."

An optical illusion or a magical phenomenon happens when a ray of light bends while going through air of various densities and different temperatures. This magical situation creates desert mirages where water and lakes seem to appear, yet in reality, there is none. Distinguishing optical illusions from reality is a quest my scientific mind, body, and soul can only complete with truth and victory.

My family and I came to Egypt as modern-day explorers on a five-day overnight camping trip. We planned to explore the pyramids and camp overnight by a pyramid that was much smaller and newer than the pyramids of Giza. Neither was this newly discovered pyramid given a name, nor was it announced to the public. It is rumored to be seen at certain times and then like the desert mirage, it disappears.

We spent the first night in the mysterious desert wide awake. We camped like we used to when my brothers and I were younger. All night, we talked about the ghost stories we had encountered as a family. My brave brothers ended up frightening themselves as they shared some of their own ghostly encounters. The funny fact though is that both my brothers married women they presumed were dead or ghosts.

Mama stopped us as she gave us the look and said, "Enough of bringing up evil from the past. Let's talk about only good people and good things, so only good shall follow, even though I know we have a lot of evil bridges to cross."

As dawn broke open, the glorious rays of the sun shined upon the glittering golden sand. We stopped talking amongst ourselves as we saw the group of people guiding us through the pyramids and the Sahara Desert approach us.

Someone amongst them said, "I don't know why we are sitting in the middle of the desert, trying to help a billionaire's personal wishes of finding a pyramid that doesn't even exist. I refuse to help. This is just taking advantage of the system because you all are a rich family. You do as you please and go places because you can afford to. We have real scientific crises we need to handle, and this is not one."

I was shocked but not too surprised at the sudden outburst of some scholars. My family and I were used to being scrutinized because of our family's social status. Everyone assumed we were the spoiled rich family, wasting money on adventures, while the inhabitants of Earth fought poverty, world hunger, and other crises. If only they had known my family members were the ones trying to fight for the people and against evil.

Mama told everyone, "Remain calm and let them say whatever they want to say. It's only words and they don't have to like our ways. We don't need to be angry at their rudeness. Words can't harm us but if we get off from our own tracks, we will be harmed in more ways than we need at this time."

The rest of the day was very mild and calm. Mysteriously, the pyramid reappeared. Some explorers who were not fond of being there couldn't see it even then. Desert hallucination also called Fata Morgana is very common.

Our hosts and the scientists who had found this pyramid all started to deny the whole story. They all said the whole thing was just a hallucination. The scientists who had sent Uncle Kees's sarcophagus now outright denied the whole event. The only person who still knew everything and did not deny the facts was Dr. Avyaan, who was involved in the top-secret project.

I wondered what or who did they think Uncle Kees was. I assumed it was good as they now wouldn't come after him calling him a vampire.

Dr. Noah Smith, a pyramidologist, who had accompanied us but was not in the confidential research group explained to us what he thought was going on.

Dr. Smith said, "I believe something very devious is going on as I have email proof of all our conversations and photos where they all acknowledged their findings. It's strange why they are now saying otherwise. They are now saying it was desert hallucination as all of them woke up with excessive heat exhaustion."

My mother walked to the group of experts that had brought us to this pyramid. The previous night, we had decided to sleep outside in the camps set for us as the cramped room inside the pyramid could maybe fit 30 people in sitting position. We experienced nothing abnormal, and we did not feel anything. My family members and Dr. Smith saw the pyramid, yet the others refused to have seen it even though they brought us to it under the guidance of Dr. Avyaan.

Mama walked back and forth as she stepped near the pyramid. Her long black hair was waving even though there was no air. Her white tunic and white pants were also blowing as if she was in a windstorm. I was so mesmerized by my mother and her inner strength. I just wanted to see what she did rather than disturb her.

My youngest brother, Andries, had other thoughts. He followed our mother and was trying to stay glued to her. Interestingly, we were all dressed identically, all in white tunics and white cotton pants as Mama does our shopping. Andries then went ahead and did what I feared he would do. He jumped and grabbed Mama.

Andries, the grown man, said in a crying voice, "Big Mama, what are you doing? Why are you walking near burial grounds by yourself? Don't you ever fear, your youngest son is here!"

Andries was sweating excessively in the desert heat and that bothered me a lot. I can never forget how my brother had walked through the door of death and came back. Even though his physical body had given up, his immortal body kept calling Mama's name. So, he walked back from being buried underground to being above the ground with Mama.

To this day, we don't know all his physical abilities because he was a miracle from the beyond. If there were any physical compromises, we were not yet aware. We know he is diabetic, and his doctor, Margriete, would never compromise his physical health. Margriete, a diabetic herself, has been treating him from his rebirth.

Margriete, Tara Bella, and Katelijne, who was his biological mother this life, walked closer to Andries as did Papa and Antonius. No one worried about Mama but all of us were a little worried about Andries. It was lovely knowing how Katelijne took everything about her son's birth so easily. She gave birth and watched him grow into a man within months. She accepted the miracle as just that a miracle.

Margriete touched Andries's forehead as she evaluated him. She stared at me in a way we both would know what she was trying to say. I understood he was completely fine and there was nothing to worry about at this time. We all sighed a sound of relief.

Mama followed all of us as she was relieved by the unspoken verses between us as she understood all of it yet said nothing. In her heart, Andries was her son who never left. As for the few months he was away, my mother almost every day slept in the graveyard by his side while she cried that he was afraid of thunder.

Mama jolted back to the current day in a blink as she said, "Tara Bella was Succubus's prisoner. She will try to attack the person who rescued her from the coffin prison in Malibu. So, my son Andries will be at risk. I prayed to Vayu, whom some know as Pavana or Vata, a Hindu God who controls the wind. I want someone to protect my son Andries from this desert weather. This paranormal weather now is being controlled by the supernatural evil Succubus and who knows if this time, we get to see Incubus, her so-called husband."

My mother was born to a Christian American father and a Hindu Indian mother. She was taught to practice all religions and taught us there is no religion, but one Creator and we are all His creation. She believes every religion should be respected as there is one common message to be good over evil.

Papa, a member of the Dutch Protestant Church, watched his wife and kissed her head and said, "Anadhi, we will all be safe and shall be fine. Remember when and where there is a war between good and evil, good always wins. Keep faith and you will see, we shall all return home safely."

My mother returned his gaze but was not fully assured by his comments. She slumped her body and moved her hands up and down as she wiped her eyes. I ran toward her as did my two brothers. We hugged her and she hugged us back.

She said, "All of you are forgetting Aunt Marinda. We must find her body and reunite her body with her spirit and time-traveling soul. We don't know how much longer she will last as her spiritual body is being separated from her physical one. If not united soon, she just might become a spirit as her body will be eternally gone."

A newcomer or a stranger's voice interrupted our morning session of trying to figure out what we were to do.

A person attired in cotton khaki drill came toward us. He had with him more people who had similar clothing on and others who had white cotton bush jackets and trousers on. He came forward as the others stayed behind and watched over all of us.

He introduced himself as Dr. Akins Ahmed. He shook Papa's hands and said he was here to help us through our dangerous adventures through the Sahara Desert.

Dr. Ahmed then in a very sharp tone said, "Dr. Jacobus Vrederic van Phillip, we have come to inform you that you have an emergency wire from Manhattan, New York in the United States of America. There is a critical surgery they need your help with. If you could be back in two weeks, then a life would be saved, a woman you all had met once. Your mother gave her a phone number to call. She will try to call you. I am assuming you know about her."

It was very strange how someone even knew I would be here. I would never decline to save a life, and I did remember Ahana Roy, a Bengali child bride whom my mother and our family had met in New York. We had met her again as my mother promised to help her. It tore my heart out how a child was being abused in New York City, yet no one even knew about her. I would do anything to save her, her young child, and the one she was carrying. I knew I would make time for it, but again I wondered how these people knew where to find me.

Dr. Ahmed said, "The message was sent from Dr. Hans Avyaan. He said you are the only one who can help. There is a child who will be sold again. She has babies who too will be sold in the dark market. They need you and your family's guidance in this situation. I don't know who this child is or how Dr. Avyaan knew you had helped the child or how she needs you all."

I promised Mr. Ahmed, "I will be in New York to perform the surgery. Please arrange for everything so I can be there. My family members will be accompanying me."

The group of army and police officers left, and the breeze too just diminished. It was as if the whole group of people came and left like an optical illusion. All was quiet and no sign of them could be heard or seen. My family members did not notice the weird way the message had arrived. Margriete contacted my eyes directly as she shivered in the extreme hot desert weather. I knew she too was worried about the third mirror. Yet again, neither Margriete nor I said anything.

Suddenly Antonius raised his voice in fear and warned everyone as he said, "Mama! Don't lean backward! The pyramid you were leaning on behind you is missing!"

My family as well as some strangers who were assisting us looked back toward the pyramid. Uncle Kees jumped up and ran toward the place where the mysterious pyramid was just standing. There was nothing but white sand. There was no sign of any building that had within its walls, sarcophagi buried.

Uncle Kees screamed, "Marinda! Please let me know where you are. I thought we were buried in the same pyramid together for life. I knew your coffin was missing, but I had hoped beyond hope I would find you buried within the same mound of Earth I was buried within. You promised to be together in life and in death."

Papa held on to his brother who looked so different from him. Papa is a six-foot-five-inch-tall Dutchman with fair skin. Uncle Kees has toffee colored skin and long raven black hair that falls to his waist. The two brothers related from a different lifetime hugged one another. I could feel the bond and love they had for one another. Nothing separated brothers. Division amongst race, color, or religion had no room in our home.

I gave the men space, and my two brothers came near me as the children stayed close to Margriete, Katelijne, and Tara Bella. Mama on the other hand walked over and stood next to Papa.

She said very softly to Uncle Kees, "As a descendant of your family lineage, I urge you to restrain to your emotions until we are all safe and know what or who we are dealing with. Remember, I do come from your side of the family."

Mama was related to Uncle Kees through her father's side. Uncle Kees had a son, but no one knew what happened to him. Mama was suddenly pointing her finger in one direction. A lake appeared in front of us. In the water, I saw Aunt Marinda was floating. How could I see this vision from so far away? It was a desert mirage. We were all seeing a lake when there was none. What about Aunt Marinda? Where did she come from?

Tara Bella then said, "It's Aunt Marinda's mirror. She is showing us a vision of some kind. We must pay attention."

We walked toward the lake and realized our mistake. The closer we walked toward the lake, the mirage too disappeared leaving us with more questions than answers. Abruptly, we heard a laughing shrieking voice who was screaming in joy as if she was going into some kind of ecstasy. We all knew this was the voice of Succubus, the demoness we had imprisoned in Malibu.

Succubus howled and said, "I will always be ahead of all you foolish humans. You really thought you could kill an immortal demoness like me."

Then again, she shrieked and laughed like she was enjoying her adventures. It felt like she was setting up the game and we were just her pawns.

Mama came close to me and said, "Jacobus, don't think like a doctor but like a paranormal family member. If she is immortal, so are we. Let the war begin."

Mama was standing in between her boys and the demoness. I realized how strong and fearless my mother is. She had always said she would be the poisonous snake everyone feared if any one of her boys were ever in danger.

As Andries held on to his wife Tara Bella who was shaking in fear, I told her, "Hey, our ember princess! You are safe within the embrace of your beloved husband's arms. This family will never allow any one of our family members to be hunted or hurt by a demoness."

That's when we all saw Uncle Kees faint. He tried to write something down on the hot desert sand. He drew a love heart and wrote, "Marinda, you are the only woman I will love, in death and in life."

I didn't know why he wrote those words at that time, but then I saw another entry appeared in the diary which read,

"My beloved, find the mirror first. It's buried somewhere in one of the pyramids here. You will not find my body here for she had it taken back to her new home near London, the home that was purchased for me for my safety by Johannes van Vrederic in the sixteenth century.

Remember, you will find a lot of mirrors. You have the one I was in. You have the medallion Succubus was in. You will also find another one with a sketch on it. Always keep that one safe and away from the demoness."

In front of my eyes, the words mysteriously disappeared as did all the sounds of a shrieking woman or any other person. I realized we must find the mirror and then we would know where to go and how.

It was getting dark again and we realized the whole day had passed by like a blur as we were searching for the missing pyramid. It was urgent for us to find some kind of shelter because the children were all tired and hungry. Darkness fell all around while we tried to scramble up some food for the children. The strangest part was only my family members were standing there as if the missing pyramid swallowed up all the others or it threw us out into a vortex where we were the only people standing. We had no food, no medicine, and no water as everything was with the people who were helping us with the tour. Astonishingly, they all disappeared.

I wondered as Succubus had appeared, maybe she placed all of us in a mirage where our guide and the people giving all of us the tour disappeared. What would they say to the world? That we just disappeared? Or would they all forget everything?

Rietje, my young daughter, started to cry as she ran to Mama and said, "Oma I am hungry, want dinner now!"

Mama tried to pick up Rietje and calm her down. At that time, I saw Griet watch Rietje, her daughter from last life and cousin from this life. She stood under the dark skies as I saw a lantern appear in her hands. Then, a basket appeared. Theunis and Alexander got up. In their hands, they had a cup and a jug.

Theunis said, "Everyone can drink from this one cup as this jug will give you what you need, not what you ask for."

Griet brought her basket which had freshly baked bread, fresh churned butter, and jam inside.

She said, "Papa Jacobus, this basket will never run out of bread. As I had promised in the sixteenth century, this bread will be provided when and only if you need it. Now please all be aware and alert. The evil woman roams around in the form of shadows. She will never give up until she has been thrown away by a power more powerful than her."

The dark desert seemed to glow under the glowing light of our girl with the lantern. I feared the unknown as I was so used to seeing everything through the eyes of a scientific scholar, not through the eyes of a son of Kasteel Vrederic. Pin-drop silence fell all around us. No one said anything, nor did anyone try to move.

We all sat in a circle as we enjoyed the bread that had been provided to the family members of Kasteel Vrederic for centuries. The bread was warm and smelled and tasted like they were freshly baked. The sweet butter was churned fresh. The smell of fresh bread gave some kind of warm comfort to my family members who were all used to being provided with these breads for centuries.

It was then we heard a very masculine voice shriek and say, "Who dare declares war with my wife? I will get rid of all of you and your dynasty until no one from your family is left in this universe. Your family tree will rot, and no one will ever remember you all even existed."

We saw a very tall man with long blond hair, fair skin, and blue eyes watch over us. I could have sworn he looked just like Theunis from his last life. Even in this lifetime, when Theunis takes an adult form, I could swear they're related.

Our young boy Theunis, the father of our Kasteel Vrederic lighthouse, just sat near Mama and was intently listening to the conversation. He gauged this new arrival and smiled with some kind of awareness, not in fear but like a conqueror, not a loser.

The demon walked like he not only was the most handsome man walking on Earth, but he was also so confident as if we were all going to be nothing but smoke with a snap of his fingers. I knew my two warriors left behind by Aunt Marinda were there as our protectors, so we had nothing to fear. Both boys neither flinched, nor did they think it was necessary for them to take their adult forms.

We were all standing in a circle near the lantern my niece had placed in the middle. The demon was smiling and inspecting our circle. He tried to snap his fingers, but nothing happened. Then, he tried to blow something from his lips, but nothing happened. We were all watching him as he kept trying to come near our small camp lit through a small lantern, yet he could not enter. Theunis and Alexander both sat at their places and started giggling.

That's when he shrieked, and I saw some desert horses appear. They were all black and came near him.

The demon then said to the horses, "My babies, go and finish them up. They have taken too much of my time. I'm tired of defending Succubus from them. She needs to be free to have all the men she wants. I could care less but I want my space and time to do as I please. I don't want to run after her. Leave the Snow White looking woman alone though. I need the sketch."

The demon laughed and examined us with some kind of fear I thought. I only wished I could have known what it was. In our circle, Theunis laughed and shook his head. He was furious. I had never seen Theunis get angry but at the teasing of the Snow White woman, he got angry. We all knew everyone compared my Margriete to Snow White.

Why was a demon scared? Or maybe the question should be what was it that he feared? Why did he keep bringing up my wife's name?

Why was Theunis laughing and why did he look so much like the demon? Oh my God, for the first time in my life, I saw Theunis resemble a demon. Theunis watched me as I knew he could read my mind. Margriete, however, went and brought Theunis closer to her like a mother would protect her children.

The demon continued speaking, "I will go back and hunt all the women I want. That's what I do. I appear to all the women who want to have sex with me. I am Incubus. The only woman I tried to have and could not is Marinda. The only man my dear Succubus wanted and could not have is Kees. But now all shall end for I will wipe you all off this Earth. I told Marinda she was free from my hunting as she could be Kees's beloved wife. I could care less."

Mama and Papa held on to one another as did Antonius and Katelijne, and Andries and Tara Bella. I held on to Margriete, Rietje, and Griet, as Margriete held with one hand Theunis and with the other hand Alexander. Uncle Kees stood up straight as he had in his hands Aunt Marinda's diary. No one said anything, not even a word. No one moved and I thought for those few minutes, the world too had frozen.

The black horses jumped toward us like crazy monsters. Then, the horses bumped into something as if there was an invisible wall. The horses bowed down like they were saluting someone inside of the circle. The horses got angry and wanted to attack their owner. The handsome demon turned ugly as his face turned hideous and for the first time he looked like a monster with rotten teeth.

I wondered who was he? A demon whose looks could be seen by everyone as he wished? Or all could see his true color when he is defeated or goes into a war? When I was a child, my mother had told me the Angel of Death could be seen as a friend if it's your time. You will want to go to him as you are attracted and then you will be dead. Or you will see his true face and be so scared that you will want to avoid him, and you will live.

Papa asked me, "Jacobus, what's going on? The demon seems angry. He is having a hard time entering our circle. Why are his horses trying to fight him and not us?"

The demon gawked at Uncle Kees as I saw the diary he held was glowing. Uncle Kees hugged his beloved wife's diary as if he wanted to hide it within his chest.

Incubus screamed, "Give me that diary! Come to me you, dreadful old diary!"

Theunis stared at the demon as he stood up and watched Incubus directly in the eyes. Alexander, the warrior of the sixteenth century, too stood next to Theunis and both young boys just stared at the demon directly. Theunis was laughing and gave a hand to Alexander as both just stood there laughing at the demon.

Incubus was becoming blind with fury as he jumped like a madman and tried to see why he couldn't come near us.

He then saw Theunis for a long time and said, "Can't be! Tell me it's not so! Why are all my demonic creatures saluting you? They do that only if we have a new ruler. Who are you?"

We all saw Theunis take his adult form as did Alexander just like they did so many times when we needed them. They would become an adult and then afterward would convert back to a child and not remember what just happened. Alexander was holding swords. He carried one in his right hand, and he carried another one in his left hand while standing in front of Theunis. It was like he was ready to fight if he needed to. Theunis looked angrily at the demonic creatures.

He shook his head, made a fist, and said, "My family members of Kasteel Vrederic follow different religious faiths. We never worship anyone but the one Creator, the God, the Omnipotent. We don't bow down to any of His creation, even if the creation has supernatural powers while humans don't. We are all creation of the Lord. Respecting and saluting a leader is okay, but don't go beyond respect and make it into worship for I would never accept it and neither should any of you."

I walked and stood next to the boys as did Papa and my brothers. As their protectors, be they old or young, we had to protect them. I knew they're different, yet I felt like I was still their guardian, and I must protect them just as I was their guardian in the sixteenth and seventeenth centuries.

Theunis, my buddy from the sixteenth century, winked at me and said, "I had given you my daughter, your granddaughter, and asked you to forever take care of her. She is now your daughter, and I told you in return, I will protect Kasteel Vrederic eternally. I have never stopped doing so, and never shall I stop protecting this home and its inhabitants. For the demon's sake, he should know at the time of my birth, he no longer is the king of the demonic world. Even if I had refused to take over or be a part of anything in the demonic world, I am who I am. I, Theunis Peters, am the only king and ruler of the demonic world through my birthright. Now all of you never, ever touch or harm my family members!"

Everyone was confused. Mama and Papa realized first. I saw Mama's eyes and I knew what she was thinking, so I told her with my eyes not to say anything. All my family members remembered at the same time that Theunis is the son of Incubus and Succubus. The family of Kasteel Vrederic, their only living bloodline, came through Alexander who was Theunis's son-in-law.

In front of everyone, a desert storm appeared and Theunis stood with his hands raised up high and said, "Incubus, my biological father hiding beneath the Earth hunting down women with sexual and demonic traits, today know I, Theunis, your biological son will stand with the people and for the people on Earth. I will protect them from all demons like you. With my birth, you know you no longer have powers to hurt or hunt my family members or me. So, it's better for you to help us and not go against us. I command you to help us and not go against us. From now on, I command all your evil strength only be used to always protect the humans on Earth and my family members."

The desert storm rose and showed its anger and fury. The desert sand was blinding everyone's vision, and it became hard to breathe without inhaling the sand. Amidst nature's fury, a father and son stood next to one another with complete opposite personalities where one was all good and one was all bad. With the birth of Theunis, the demonic world no longer could hunt down any one of us nor did they have power to hunt down Theunis.

Good ruled over bad just like Mama and Papa had said. Why was Succubus still fighting us? Did she go even against the rules of the demonic world? She probably would as I would not put it against her character.

Theunis was smiling as he saw Alexander gaze at him and he said, "Always remember my blessed warrior, above all demons and evil is the love and the blessed prayers and touches of good. I found that within the walls of Kasteel Vrederic. Promises and vows I had taken will last and keep my family members and all the humans on Earth safe as long as they believe in good over bad. Also, Incubus or whatever your name is, never ever look at or ask for Margriete who is the mother I had accepted, not just mother-in-law. Don't ever look for the mirror with the sketch."

The promises and demands made from a son of a demon were heard by only the demon Incubus and the Kasteel Vrederic family members who were all his lineage. No one other than the invisible staircase that was linked from the Sahara Desert to the skies above was our witness. We knew everyone above the skies and beneath the Earth too heard the vows of the man who was the new ruler and the son of the demon. Here our other witness forever shall be the miraculous and mysterious Sahara Desert.

SAHARA DESERT

You the mysterious desert

Span across

9,200,000

Square kilometers.

Across eleven

Different countries,

You have written your

Mysterious tales.

You have built

Within your chest

In Egypt,

Some of the

Famous pyramids which are

Burial grounds of

The pharaohs,

The known

And unknown

Lost citizens

Who once roamed

Within Earth,

Yet sleep

Now within your tombs.

Within your chest,

WOMAN IN THE MIRROR: VOWS FROM THE BEYOND

You have kept

A very special soul

Protected and sealed

From the world

Yet now is missing.

With your mystical powers,

Guide us

To the place

We need to be within.

Tell us the stories

That are buried

Within your chest,

The mysteries

We all need to hear

Yet have not.

Tell us,

Share with us

Mysteries that

Are looming around

And are hidden

Within your chest

Oh, the

Enchanted,

Numinous,

Mysterious

SAHARA DESERT.

CHAPTER THREE:

INCUBUS THE DEMON

"Like Father
Is not the son,
As character traits
Are not defined
By blood,
But through nurture,
And is drawn
Through love."

The great Sahara Desert has written so many love stories over time. If only the desert sand could speak and retell all the love stories it has witnessed, then we would have tales to last us eternally. Each day a new story is being retold and is being redrafted.

Uncle Kees and Aunt Marinda's love story never found its pages, nor was it bound in a book. A storm had appeared and blew away all the pages of their love story which found no listeners to accept the story. Yet there were two lovers who never let go, nor did they forget one another.

Before the storm called Incubus had entered our life, I had read a part of Aunt Marinda's diary. In the early sixteenth century, when witch burnings and hangings were normal, a witch was hung at the gallows. She was innocent. Her only crime was that her niece was jealous of her beauty. The niece testified against her own aunt. The niece in this story was the demoness Succubus and the aunt, the accused witch who was hung at the gallows, was Aunt Marinda.

Aunt Marinda had rescued Tara Bella, my beautiful sister-in-law and Andries's beloved wife, and kept her alive for centuries, only for Andries to be reborn and rescue her. Yet what about Aunt Marinda's own love story, which never found life? She never spoke about it, but only kept on being of service to all who needed her.

My thoughts were broken as I realized my family and I were still in a circle protecting ourselves from the dark demon Incubus. He stood up and it was as if he was in some kind of transformative state. He watched Theunis like he was in a hex. I knew the demon was traveling time and could check everything before we could even blink. Time traveling was something Aunt Marinda did too and had saved our lives so many times through this gift of hers.

Incubus opened his eyes, looked at Theunis, and said, "You, Theunis Peters, are my only living son. I should have known. There is no one living or dead on or above the universe who has the powers to stop me, except for any bloodline of mine. You just by being born have taken over my kingdom. I wonder why it is that I had still ruled if this demonic world knew of your birth."

Incubus calmed down or I felt like he knew he was just defeated by the only person he could be defeated by. As he sat on a huge black horse, I saw the horse drop him on the ground. The horse became a half man and a half horse and saluted Theunis. The horse man brought a bowl of water from somewhere and left the bucket. We all watched a red rose grow inside of it. Then, we all saw in the hot desert, a rose tree had grown bearing red roses. Around the rose tree appeared a fountain. The water was bubbling and looked almost like a glass mirror rather than water.

Incubus smiled and said, "I see now you rule, and I have been defeated. So, why is it you had let me live all these years? Even though you knew it is you who are the king of all demons. You accept or don't, matters not for they will only listen to you. I was very careful not to have a sire because I like to rule and don't like it if I must step down. I will never object for as you know, if I do, then my physical body will be no more."

Incubus stood there mesmerized, or frozen at the news he had received without realizing what was going on. He laughed and tried to walk but we saw he could barely move or do anything.

He again observed his son as he laughed out loud and said, "That's why Succubus is changing bodies and can't have the same body for more than one lifetime. She did not accept you or your terms to be good, so she left. She is a fool as she does not realize she only can live by entering other people's bodies. So, she has been killing for centuries. She is just not a sex demoness but a killer."

Incubus tried to get on his horse, but the horse knocked him off again.

He said directly to his son, "Through you, my only family, our enemy has created their blood lineage too. So, it seems like we are related. The Kasteel Vrederic family and we are all related through blood. I don't understand why Succubus would go to so much length to fight and get Kees when he belongs to another woman. I saw Marinda actually protect you, Theunis, from being murdered by Succubus. Succubus wanted to get Kees and through him, she wanted to control the Kasteel Vrederic household and get you back. Alas, you married the daughter of a human, Jacobus van Vrederic. You fell for good, and I assume became a good demon. That's admirable, but yuck! That's so disgusting for our world!"

Papa and Uncle Kees stood up and held on to one another as Uncle Kees said, "Theunis was Marinda's bloodline. She knew how he was dumped and left to die by his own mother the demoness. So, Marinda swore she would raise Theunis to be good, with or without any powers he might have had from birth. Marinda didn't care whether she had or didn't have any magical powers, but only love which is the most powerful weapon in any world."

The desert weather became extremely frigid as it was freezing at night. Griet and Rietje started to cry as they felt cold. Theunis clicked his fingers and I saw the lantern became a huge fire. He saw the two girls and told something to them through telepathy. It was so strange as I knew Incubus understood what he had said. Margriete held the girls as did Mama. Theunis stood in the way so Incubus could not even try to harm the girls.

Incubus laughed for a while when he said, "I am known to be a sex maniac, and I do go and enter dreams of people who invite me only. I will not harm my own son who is now the King. If I do, I will be vanished like ashes. I'd rather like to live like a demon and not harm anyone if that's the way I get to live. You are the King and even if you believe or do not believe, I will never allow Succubus or anyone to become an obstacle for you Theunis or Alexander, for through your bloodline, we can be defeated anytime, anywhere."

Antonius and Andries came and stood by me as I stood by Papa and Uncle Kees. It was all strange as the demoness who was trying to harm Uncle Kees and Aunt Marinda was the same woman who helped the lineage of the Kasteel Vrederic family to continue.

I told Incubus, "Theunis is in no way like you or your demoness wife Succubus, as we, who have reincarnated from the lineage of Theunis, are in no way linked to you, nor do we want you or your likes to ever be linked to any one of us. Theunis is our son and will always be ours. We don't rule through power but good versus bad."

I felt Incubus was a demon who did not want to be bad or was not as bad as we had assumed. Somehow, he seemed different.

Incubus then said, "Although I am a demon, and I have many immoral traits inside of me, I again swear I will never become a hindrance for my only son, the King who chose good against bad. If he chooses to be virtuous, then let him have my blessings to be only noble. I will return to my world where everyone, even though are all demons and demonesses, will always do as Theunis wishes. Never will they go or be able to go against him. Even if we so want to, we will become ashes like dust and we will burn within the rays of the sun."

We all noticed Incubus gazed at his only son and somehow had seen our past lives in a blink. He was worried and it exhibited on his face. He did something with his hands. In the fountain that had appeared, the water that looked like a mirror became a mirror. The rose tree was glistening inside of the mirror.

The amazing red roses turned white and within the mirror appeared a woman, the most beautiful woman I had ever seen in my life. She smiled at us, and we all knew who the beautiful woman was. She was beautiful, she was graceful, and she was our own, Aunt Marinda.

Incubus said, "This is my gift to you. You will always know where she is, and she can travel to and from anywhere she wants as long as she travels through the mirror. Do remember I cannot take away nor can I erase the curses of Succubus. You need to find Marinda's body and make sure she returns as a bride of Kasteel Vrederic."

Mama was standing there and for some reason she did not fear anyone as she stood up and looked directly into the eyes of Incubus. She wanted to ask something, but it was as if she was hesitant.

All I heard was Incubus say, "I believe you are a direct lineage from Marinda's side. No, I did not have her hung neither did I separate Kees and Marinda. You will find their separation tale in the loose pages in the mirror with Marinda. I gift you this mirror which does have her soul hidden in it. You must find her body for then and only then she will be free. Also, try to find the mirror with the sketch as soon as possible. It's different from the medallion or the mirror or mirrors Marinda was in."

Incubus, the demon, stared at Griet and Rietje. As he tried to touch them, his hands got burned. He smirked and tried again but could not. Griet scrutinized him with her little body and jumped on top of my lap. She hid her face inside of my chest. I saw Theunis was angry at this gesture Incubus made. Griet was the love of Theunis's life who had with her love made Theunis the only demon on Earth and beyond to become an angel in human disguise. Andries walked past me and wanted to go and punch the demon.

He screamed with fury and said, "You leave her alone! In this life, she is my sister! Rietje is my cousin! I'm not scared of you or that sex freak Succubus. She can go to Hell or beyond, I don't care. Just leave my family alone."

Andries and Antonius probably would go and fight this demon as would Papa and Mama. My entire family was ready to fight the demon when he gave Griet and Rietje the stare. My tolerant family loses all of their patience when and where Griet and Rietje are involved. No one gives them any kind of stare and remains standing to hear the end of the story.

Incubus just laughed. He was laughing so hard that I thought the desert sand would all evaporate, and we would all become invisible within a whirling storm of laughter. He came as close to the circle as he could. Theunis and Alexander too went closer to the line without crossing the line.

Theunis had drawn a line around our family. He was in control, not Incubus. Theunis smiled and watched the demon as his long blond hair blew in the cold freezing desert night's air. The temperature variations made it feel so much colder than it was in the morning.

Our Theunis feared nothing as he said, "Don't get out of the circle at any cost, not even if you feel like I'm dead. I had placed myself within the coffin of my wife and have through love become immortal, yet I thought at the time I was going to be dead. That was all right for in life or in death, remember Griet, we will be together."

I wanted to shout at my little boy who was standing in front of us like a thirty-year-old man. The sounds froze in my mouth when I saw Theunis walk outside of the line. He went and touched the demon on his shoulder. Suddenly, I felt like two Theunises were standing in front of us. Somehow though, I could still tell the difference.

Margriete who raised him in this life and was close to him in her last life screamed, "Please my baby boy, don't do anything that would hurt this mother of yours. I am your mother. It matters not who gave birth to you."

Theunis stood head-to-head with the demon as they just stared one another down.

As Theunis raised his fire-lit sword toward the demon, Incubus said, "Ahh so you do have some of me inside of you. You want to defend your twin flame Griet and your child from last life, Rietje. Yet you forget I too am Rietje's grandfather. Griet was my daughter-in-law. I just want to bless them, not curse them."

There was a shrieking sound in the air as we all looked up and knew Succubus was coming. I wondered how she managed to travel lands apart in this life without being noticed by anyone. That too after she was kicked out of her demonic world. She rules and runs her own game her own way.

Incubus glanced at all of us and in a very worried voice said, "I will protect you all from wherever I am or might be. Even if I don't want to, I have to abide by these rules. I am evil and I won't argue with that. I am proud my son and his lineage are good. My son rules the beyond and even though he does not accept them, they will never let him fall. So maybe somewhere inside of me I too have a good side. I am his father. Okay, fine. So, I don't have any good but am selfish and do this as that's the only way I get to live my life."

Incubus kept staring at the skies above. Uncle Kees followed his gaze and starred at the skies as he looked worried and tried to figure out what was going on. Papa held on to Griet and Rietje in his chest. He carried the two girls as they quietly hid their faces inside of him.

Papa said, "They only have one grandfather and that's me. Any other person trying to say anything otherwise should just leave."

I felt like there was something Incubus, the night demon, was hiding. I wondered how was all this possible? The demon known as a folklore who only preys upon sleeping women was standing in front of us. He was no folklore but the hidden truth behind my family and our lineage. I knew Theunis had hated his father and mother but never knew why. Now we all knew why.

Incubus laughed out loud and was shrieking like his female counterpart. They were both very similar but somehow different. I tried to read his facial expressions.

I heard Uncle Kees sit down on the desert sand. His black hair was blowing in the desert breeze that made everything feel so much cooler. Uncle Kees was inspecting the shadows of ancient structures all around us. The skies above were warning all of us darkness would evolve soon. The desert would reveal all the hidden ghosts shortly. We were all just waiting in anticipation of what laid ahead of us.

Uncle Kees sighed and said, "Don't think of anything as he can read minds. Stay focused and think of nothing."

The desert winds were singing some kind of a horror song. The musical notes were digging into our skin, it felt like desert cactuses spiking through our skin.

Incubus watched all of us and said, "Erasmus van Phillip or the original Johannes van Vrederic, don't fear. I will never come and claim my family lineage or my granddaughter, even though Rietje and now the lineage that came from her are all from my son, Theunis."

Our brave warrior, who was standing tall as a young man walked forward and had his hands clenched in a fist. He watched Alexander who stood next to him waiting for Theunis to say what to do and would go confront the demon head on. Both young men were blocked off by my mother.

Incubus was either smirking or afraid, I could not tell his facial attributes as he stared at her and said, "No need to worry about me. I might be sexually deranged, but I will never harm my own bloodline even though I can't guarantee that about my female counterpart. She is not just sexually deranged but evil even in my standards. I lost her as she chose to be a bloodsucking demoness. She walked out of our world as she refused to live by the rules."

I watched Incubus and knew he feared something as he kept staring at the skies above. My mother who was not afraid of saying the wrong thing even to the demon came in front of me and almost walked out of the circle that Theunis drew.

Incubus screamed and said, "Don't walk out of the circle that protects you even from me and Succubus! We can't harm or fight our own son. He by birth has all our combined powers and by giving up all bad and choosing to be good and by burying himself in the same coffin of his beloved, he became the protector of Kasteel Vrederic and its lineage forever. Don't even by mistake trust me without talking everything over with Theunis."

I realized the story that began our journey with all the diaries were now coming to life. I watched my brave warrior Theunis and realized how much he loved Griet that he gave up eternity eternally for her.

Incubus said again, "I will try to be a helping hand by keeping you all safe from being attacked by Succubus. Remember she will try to keep Marinda hidden in the ancient stone circle called Stonehenge. It's about 150 kilometers west of London which you should know is older than the pyramids of Egypt. There is a mirror hidden in that diary which Kees has in his hands. Don't trust your Dr. Avyaan, as he is not everything you think him to be. He too wants the mirrors, all the mirrors. That was the only reason he too wanted you all to come here. He won't remember anything as he too is in her control. This diary will guide you to Marinda. Don't even by mistake think about the mirror with the sketch, with any one of us. Forget about it, Jacobus."

Like a storm, he was gone and there were only his warnings left written on the desert sand. The writing glowed in the dark. Written were whispers of a demon. A demon father was overjoyed how from the house of demons was born a good-hearted warrior who saved lives and did not take lives. I knew our story too would be stored amongst all the stories that were lived but bound in a diary and found only in the library of Kasteel Vrederic. The night's cold and harsh winds would tomorrow whisper our dark stories of the night to all the visitors of the Sahara Desert.

I walked and picked up my daughter and niece as they were watching and listening to all the horrific details yet like children, they said nothing.

We read the letter that began to appear on the sand as if the words were burned on to the sand.

"Dear family I consider, even though I know you will never, and that too makes me feel good, I came here to wipe all of you out of this universe. When I saw Rietje's eyes, I knew she is related to me by blood. Half human and half demon blood run in her body. No, I don't talk about your reincarnated Rietje today, but the one who continued your dynasty. This Rietje is here because of the original one. My son Theunis's bloodline.

I wonder, have I angered you yet, Theunis, by calling you, my son? No, I don't think you know how to be angry. It felt good how from evil not always will be born evil. Jacobus had raised Rietje, an angel, then and today you all have from that same good angel's bloodline returned.

Like the lighthouse on top of your castle, I too will always keep you all safe from Succubus and all other evil that roam around. It's true it takes an evil to catch an evil. Don't hate me for who I was created to be, an evil demon, as your Lord and mine created me but I never gave myself a chance to be good. You can, however, choose to decline me and my deceptions anytime.

I am known as a demon who the world calls Incubus."

The words faded as they appeared on the desert sand. It felt warm when the letters were appearing. I can only compare the appearance of the words like someone was writing a letter through fireworks, yet there was just light and no sounds.

I stood on the desert sand as I wondered where the pyramid that had Uncle Kees's sarcophagus buried within vanished to. Another letter started to appear again lit with fireworks. The letter read as follows,

"Oops sorry Jacobus, I forgot to mention. I had wiped out the unnamed pyramid Kees was buried within from this Earth. Now without the pyramid that ties Succubus to Kees, she has no ties left with him. You can thank me Kees as I set you free from her captivity. Eternally you are free and yes, you are immortal. You will need a coffin to sleep in though at nights, so you stay immortal.

I am not reading your mind Jacobus, but maybe I am! You will never know. You see doctors are always skeptical about the paranormal world. So, it's easy to read your mind. Hardest is your mother's. I read her mind only when she allowed me to do so.

I am again warning you all to find Marinda quickly and always keep the mirror close to you. Ahh, you wonder which one? You will know when you finally find it. Maybe your mother can hold on to it as I can't enter her thoughts so neither can Succubus if she keeps her mind blocked.

I do wish to find out the secret as to why I can't enter your mind or read your thoughts Anadhi Newhouse van Phillip without your permission. Maybe because you come from Marinda's bloodline.

All of you stay together and keep the children with you always. The new children you will adopt, Tara Bella, keep them closer. I do know you were a prisoner of Succubus and so you won't conceive children of your own. She takes away those abilities from her prisoners. You should know she is a very jealous demoness, however, if you all can save the two girls from another Earthly demon, then they will be yours. They wait for you in New York City. Go there soon Jacobus as one of Tara Bella's children need you to even be born.

Please know this is my way of apologizing for Succubus and her ruthless atrocities against my own family. Yes, I can hear someone's screams as you are screaming in your head saying you are not my family. It's all right. I actually don't take any of your rudeness and anger as insults. I am an expert at insulting any or everyone, so it just does not bother me. I am glad you too can be so mean in your minds even though you are not brave enough to utter the words from your lips.

Take care everyone,

Incubus"

Again, the words disappeared just as they had appeared. No one said anything except Theunis who screamed, "I am not your son Incubus! You are made from fire, and I am not. How could I be your son?"

Theunis's words did bother me, but I kept my thoughts to myself. If Succubus and Incubus are made from fire, then how is he now or even in the past was a human with great powers? He must have always been powerful without knowing it. Or he had chosen to decline the powers or had controlled them.

My mother went to Theunis and hugged him. He started to shift and become a child again. Mama's eyes told me she knew much more, but she kept quiet which was not her character. Mama could read my mind. Even when I was a child, she would give me a look and I knew she heard all my thoughts.

She was laughing as she said, "Yes, I can read minds Jacobus, but only sometimes. Not just your mind but your father's and both of your brothers. I can't read the minds of anyone else yet."

Margriete held Theunis from the other side and said, "Theunis is half human. Succubus the demoness uses human bodies to bid all her evil activities, even sex. This is just my thought. Remember Theunis was born from a human woman's womb who was possessed by the demoness."

Mama tenderly smiled at Theunis as he was a child now. She picked him up in her arms and carried him like she had carried my brothers and me when we were children. I started to laugh in my head as I wondered how the small petite woman had carried all of us even when we were so much older. She looked so big then and now it hurts me to think how I allowed her to do it. Mama and Papa gave me the look as they were both annoyed at me.

Papa said, "I thought demons can't get the satisfaction of sex as they can never complete it or have orgasms. So, they use human bodies to do their desires. I feel like Succubus and Incubus both used two human individuals to have sex and those humans gave birth to Theunis. So, he became a human with some of their powers. Yes, he had the human traits of his biological parents, not just the demons who took over the bodies."

Theunis now was hugging Papa as he smiled and was happy to have the human traits. I knew Theunis was a brave and blessed human boy with powers passed on to him from Succubus and Incubus which he passed on to all of us through his marriage to Griet. The Kasteel Vrederic family tree now had the traits of Succubus and Incubus the demon.

INCUBUS THE DEMON

Good versus evil,

The war

Began in Heaven above,

And still exists

On Earth beneath.

The human

I am,

As are you,

Who have the power

To change a child

Into a blessed son

Or a blessed daughter

Through nourishing love, faith,

And belief in science and reality,

Versus what we see

Yet is not there.

Bad dreams are like

Desert mazes.

They feel and seem real

Yet fade away

At the first

Sight of dawn.

Prophesy dreams

Are given

To the blessed,

To the seekers,

And to the psychics

To see and protect

Their families

To remove

Obstacles and to be

The guiding stars

Of the desert skies.

Believe in dreams,

Not nightmares,

For when the differences

Are realized,

The warriors,

The stars, and

The good humans are identified.

The dark desert skies

Can't hide the evil as

Where there is evil,

There is always good.

The warriors

Who were born

To fight evil

Even though

These stars,

Might have been

Born from the house of

The evil demon,

Known to you,

And to all

As

INCUBUS THE DEMON.

CHAPTER FOUR:

STONEHENGE

"Dark secrets whisper
In the air
For you to unveil them
As they hide themselves
In the world's
Prehistoric structures
Such as the
Stonehenge."

ear gripped the beautiful and quaint English town of Amesbury as a woman was hunting down the young men and women of this town. This busy vibrating area attracts millions of visitors yearly. All attractions are attributed to the ancient landscapes which include the nearby famous heritage site, the Stonehenge. The breathtaking ancient stone circle is older than the pyramids we just visited. This town's history dates back to 8820 B.C.

My family and I came here to meet Dr. Avyaan who worked in London, about two hours away from his home in Amesbury. Something or someone was hunting down the citizens of London all the way to Amesbury which is located on the Salisbury Plain. The citizens near the Stonehenge and the visitors all locked their doors and windows to keep this evil demonic woman from entering their homes. All the hotels and the small cottages where visitors normally flocked to were empty. Tourists were staying away from this town or nearby towns as a precautionary measure.

Precautions were being taken against an unknown and unseen supernatural demonic woman. Seen only by the eyes of her victims, no one survived to give any description of their slayer. We were invited to stay with Dr. Avyaan in his family home, but we decided to stay on our own. We walked into our small vacation villa near the famous historical site. As the sun burst open in the amazing skies, it did not feel like we were walking into a horror movie set like what was described over the phone by Dr. Avyaan. I was worried what he actually wanted, yet I kept my feelings to myself.

Margriete was sitting next to Mama who was driving the camper we rented from the airport. Papa decided to get one so if we wanted, we could park and stay inside the camper. It was safer for us traveling with children even though we left all our luggage in the rental cottage. We read there was a nice camping ground near our targeted visiting site.

Mama was talking with Margriete quietly as she laughed out loud and said, "Mama, I completely agree with you. If we happen to be lucky and get a sunny and clear day, we might see blue jet lightning in front of us."

As everyone joined in on the joke, we knew the fear very visible in Margriete's voice was real. Even if everyone missed it, I did not. Papa walked in the camper back and forth trying to calm the kids by bribing them with personalized Toblerone milk chocolate bars, honey, and almond nougats he got from Heathrow Airport.

It worked not only with the kids but with all the women and my brothers too. Even Mama was busy with her bar. She didn't open hers as it would ruin her name written on the bar. So, I gave her mine to eat and told her to save hers for later. I got a big kiss from Mama for the gesture. For Andries and Margriete, Papa had specially made sugar-free ones like he always does as they are both diabetic.

Astonishingly I saw for the first time in my life, blue jet lightning. Although it's a rare sighting, it does happen. On a very sunny day where there were no sights of any storm happening near us, appeared colorful flashes ejecting into the stratosphere. A thunder cloud probably took place about a hundred miles away. The lightning struck the Stonehenge.

We were all still attired in all white clothing as we only had desert clothing with us since this trip was not on our itinerary. On top of the Stonehenge circle, was floating a woman dressed all in black. The sight was so eerie that it could awaken the dead and would probably kill the living, not in fear, but because Succubus is utterly so ugly.

The silence broke when we heard Tara Bella scream in fear, "Oh my God, she is back. She will take me back and imprison me again. Aunt Marinda, please help!"

Tara Bella, a very terrified and startled woman, started to cry. Her husband Andries, my youngest brother, held on to her.

He said, "Don't you dare cry or fear any woman who is scared to be dead that she hunts living humans and sucks their life out to stay alive. You are brave. We don't fear even death, so what else is there to fear?"

Margriete got the four children as Papa took over the driving from Mama who stood up and said, "Like the desert illusions, she is also performing some kind of optical illusion. She is a spirit who needs a living body to do her biddings. She is weak and senile, but she is not powerful. Don't ever fear the weak for all the evil on this Earth and beyond are evil because they fell prey to their own weakness."

With all of us in our camper, we rushed back to Dr. Avyaan due to some mysterious sightings and gruesome murders. We received phone calls from Dr. Avyaan saying all the murder victims had one thing in common. A note was left with their lifeless bodies.

The message read,

"KASTEEL VREDERIC FAMILY MEMBERS, I WANT THE DIARY WITH THE MIRROR. GIVE BACK MY MIRROR OR I WILL

GIVE YOU MORE LIFELESS BODIES. NO
NEGOTIATIONS. I WANT THE MIRROR YOU
WILL FIND AND KNOW I WILL HUNT YOU
DOWN TO GET IT."

Dr. Avyaan invited us to his private home to discuss this issue as now my family name had been dragged to the gruesome murder sites. How could we give a diary that belongs to my family without exposing my family history we didn't want to share publicly?

We entered Dr. Avyaan's private residence, which was very close to the Stonehenge historical site. The stone cottage looked cold and bare. There were no flowers growing like Dr. Avyaan likes or had at the lab in the Vrederic Hospital. There were no butterflies. No birds sang around the amazing stone cottage which could have been like a small paradise if only there was some curb appeal. Mama said it out loud as she never can keep her thoughts inside.

She halted in place and in disbelief whispered, "Such a gloomy and forbidding atmosphere. It gives me a do not enter warning signal. I don't want to enter, but I know that's the only reason we need to enter. I feel like someone doesn't want us to enter. I have a feeling Dr. Avyaan knows much more than what he has shared with us."

Somehow Mama was right. I couldn't link this house to our Dr. Avyaan. Something was amiss, and it brought shivers to my spine. I knew that's the only reason we should enter. My mother always told me as a child, a demonic house always pulls you to it. The flowers will bloom, the house will feel relaxing, yet something will feel shady. I didn't know where this house stood in the list.

Margriete is usually very calm, and I had rarely seen her panic in our entire wedded life. Nevertheless, she stayed very close to me and held my hands. She carried Rietje in her arms as Katelijne carried Griet. Tara Bella took Alexander as Mama carried Theunis. I followed the children and the women, and wondered was it their motherly intuition or our psychic family's transmitters going up?

The weirdest part was my two brothers Antonius and Andries held Papa's two hands as they both looked very worried at the worst times and hours. I didn't know if I should laugh or cry at their behavior. They amused me even at the oddest times.

Uncle Kees touched my back as he gestured me to look up. In the sky on top of the roof was floating Incubus. Dressed all in black, he winked at us. Some might think he looked cool. I thought he looked strange as a grown-up man was playing dress up in a vampire gown. I knew, though, he was the real vampire.

The demon was watching over us as we knocked on the door of the stone cottage. A fair European woman in her mid-forties with brown hair answered the door. Her eyes were somewhat lost in a daze. As a doctor, I wondered if she was all right or was going to faint or doze off.

She was extremely rude and furious as she shouted, "Who the hell are you? Why are you all knocking on my door? Please don't park your camper on my yard or my parking lot. Now, whoever you may be, leave my property or I will call the cops. You all are giving me a headache. I am being asked to tell you all to leave."

She was staring at Uncle Kees. I thought she forgot everything and was just watching him. I could swear she had tears fall from her eyes but then like a rude woman or machine, she waltzed around and wanted to close the door. She bruised herself trying not to close the door. I wondered if she was fighting herself, her memories, or was just pretending to be evil.

Papa who was not used to rude people saying no to him used the same tone and said, "I am Erasmus van Phillip, who has employed your husband Dr. Avyaan in my hospital.

I would like a minute of his time if it's not really bothering you."

She saw Papa as if she was mesmerized and didn't move for a while. She said something but no words came out of her mouth. Then, she turned red as she screamed back at him even louder. I wondered how a person could shout so rudely to the employer of her husband. Mama, however, was calm, and I knew because she is a psychic, she knew more than we saw or knew.

Mama, a small petite half-Indian and half-American woman with long black hair went in front of Papa and said, "Lower your voice woman because you will otherwise lose more than you will gain. We have a friend with us who you probably know and are familiar with who is watching over us. We didn't come here on our own, but we were invited to come. As you must know, invited guests can enter the house of demons as the demons can enter houses they are invited to enter. My son, Jacobus, wants to talk to you for a few minutes."

The woman said with tears in her eyes some words, and her voice sounded so familiar, but I couldn't grasp the whole of it.

I thought I heard her say, "Jacobus, help me please. I am scared as I can't control myself."

Suddenly the woman walked backward as she saw something in Mama's eyes. She then sat down on her very old and torn couch. The house was decorated like the outside of the house looked. The carpets were torn, and the walls had ivies growing inside. The ceiling had water damage. The windows were all broken but covered in vines. So, the broken glass was not visible from outside, nor were any windows or broken glasses visible inside as ivies were growing even inside. It was just through the ivies there were some gaps, and you could tell there were broken windows.

The small family room opened to the small kitchen which had a fresh pot of tea brewing inside. Griet jumped off her mother's arms and placed a basket of fresh bread on the worn-out kitchen table. Like a charmed house, there appeared more baskets of fresh bread. Then, we saw tea appeared for everyone. Griet never did this in any stranger's home. I wondered why she was doing this so easily, without anyone asking her anything. She volunteered to do this.

Griet said like a child would, "I am hungry. So, I made bread and milk for us and tea for you Papa Jacobus. I love you, Papa Jacobus."

I kissed my goddaughter, my niece, and daughter from last life, and as I hugged her in my chest, I told her "My heart beats Griet and Rietje."

A famous sentence we always said in all our incarnations. The strange woman trembled as she looked me in the eye and whispered again, "Jacobus."

Griet went and kissed the woman as if she was not afraid of the screaming and shouting woman. She and Rietje sat next to her as they broke bread and fed her with their tiny hands. We all realized the woman had not eaten in days as she went and helped herself with the loaf of fresh bread the girls were feeding her. She also took a cup of tea. She sat down as I watched my wife Margriete go sit next to her. I realized the doctor inside of Margriete woke up and started to check the woman.

Margriete said, "She is dehydrated and has not eaten properly. She needs to eat slowly and needs medical assistance, Jacobus. She is angry and rude because her blood pressure is high, and her vitals are not good. We need to get her help but don't want anyone to know about her."

Margriete and I became doctors as we started giving her basic medical treatments immediately. I called for medical assistance as we helped transport and admit her to the Vrederic Hospital London secretly and treated her in a very secure area in the hospital where Dr. Avyaan too worked in. What was out of place was that Dr. Avyaan never came, even though we had let him know that his wife was in the hospital being treated for dehydration and starvation.

We all waited for her as she recovered in the hospital. I walked in with Margriete as my family members waited for us at the stone cottage. That evening, the woman woke up from her much-needed sleep. We brought her back home as she welcomed our family to her home.

We wanted to leave and go back to the park where we had stayed with our camper. The children were all looking forward to the park and camping vacation, yet we had another twist to our work vacation.

The woman we knew as Mrs. Alice Hans Avyaan said, "I don't know why you had said my husband talked with you a few days ago. It made me angry as my husband had passed away years ago. People still come asking for him. I don't know why at times I don't know who I am and why I have come here or how. I know someone said the name Alice and so I assumed I am her."

Mama went to Papa as she held his hands. Andries and Antonius, my brave brothers, went to Mama and held her from behind. They always did that even as children. They would both either get on Mama's lap or hide behind her. Antonius was blind at birth, so Mama always carried him, and Papa carried Andries who was his twin. I watched them and had to smile from the fun memories.

I looked at Alice and wondered how I would break to her the news. Her husband was not dead for we saw him a few days ago and he invited us to his house now. As a doctor, I had to break bad news and give good news to so many patients. I strive to switch all bad news into good news. I must do it again, but I didn't know if this was good or bad news. Also, why was Incubus still standing on top of the roof?

Alice watched all of us and said, "I keep on seeing dreams of a man I assumed was Hans. He had passed away in the horrific car crash near the Stonehenge, but I saw he was scared of a woman. He said the woman hunted him and was tormenting him to do something for her. He said it had something to do with the Kasteel Vrederic family. He refused to give out any information to the woman who claimed she was a demoness."

My family members began to look at one another and said nothing. We all knew something wasn't right. Mama, the dream psychic, watched the woman who was recovering from extreme dehydration and starvation as if she realized something. I wondered if her husband had been dead for two years, then the question would be, how long had she been like this? Who had been providing her with food and water?

Uncle Kees walked over and sat next to the woman and said, "Why is it that you look so familiar, as if I know you? Who are you? I promised under any circumstances, in any way, and anyhow, I would recognize you. I feel like I want to, but you are going away, and I am having a hard time with it."

The woman somehow was staring at Uncle Kees like she too knew him. Her eyes were glued on his eyes for a long time. She jumped up from the sofa like she was mad or upset at him. She kept glancing at the roof, and we knew at that time she was afraid of whatever was on the roof. At the same time, Katelijne and Antonious came and showed me something they found on the internet.

Mama watched all of us and said, "Just say it out loud. He can hear and read your thoughts anyway."

I watched my family and told them to be quiet. I saw Mrs. Avyaan or the woman who claimed to be Mrs. Avyaan fall asleep. I carried her with help from Antonius and left her in her bed. She was weak and felt very tired as if she was asleep for centuries, not for two years. Somehow, she reminded me of Uncle Kees when he had walked out from the sarcophagus. I then asked Antonius to explain what he and Katelijne found.

Antonius told everyone, "Dr. Avyaan had passed away two years ago. The newspaper article states that as the famous doctor had discovered two sarcophagi, one buried in Egypt and one in the Stonehenge in England, he met up with his own death. His car burned to ashes, but his body was untouched by the fire. It is said he died immediately. No cause of death was recorded. A very strange accident. He never married nor did he have any family members who claimed his body. So, no one knows what happened to his physical body."

I wondered if Dr. Avyaan had passed away, then who is the Dr. Avyaan who has been helping us with our investigations? Abruptly we heard a strange shriek come from the great Stonehenge area. A woman was screaming and all the residents around the area were trying to get out of this area. People thought we were being invaded by people from outer space. Instead of looking into what was going on, people were blaming the government for lying about aliens.

I told my family members, "Let's get a grip and not run with the crowd. Remember, we always run against the crowd in paranormal activities. Also, if Dr. Avyaan never married, who is this woman claiming to be Mrs. Avyaan?"

Through the windows, we had a clear sight of the Stonehenge. Its story and all the mysteries leading to this stone circle date back nine thousand years. I watched the prehistoric structure and tried to talk to it. What if it is alive and knows much more than we do? It was standing to witness all the mysteries. Maybe it could replay them for us.

I feared for my brave family members. I knew they were all trying to be brave as we waited for an answer from somewhere.

I asked out loud, "Oh great prehistoric structure, could you guide us to the answers? People have said you have within your chest so many mysteries. You stand like an ancient stone circle, yet I know you are a portal to something. Maybe the secret we seek is hidden within your walls as you are an ancient heritage site. The world has named you the Stonehenge."

STONEHENGE

How and why

Were you built,

As you are

But older than

The pyramids of Giza?

Are you

Like the pyramids,

A sacred burial ground,

Or do you cherish

Within your body

Sacred, cremated ashes?

Or are you

The devil's playground?

You remind us

Of a woman's

Fertility ground.

Or are you the witches'

Time traveling

Crystal fort?

I sit and wonder,

Why were you built?

Do you hide

The world's

Healing powers?

Your creators are unknown,

As are your

Sacred chambers,

Which might

Be a connecting

Invisible bridge,

Or the crossing ground

For the spirits who exist,

Who can see us,

Who can feel us, and

Make us do things

We don't know.

However powerful

Your magnets or forces

Might be,

You still need

Us the humans

For your actions

May they be good

Or may they be bad.

So, it comes down to

We, the humans, must

Be more powerful

Than just your

Stone walls

As you can't breathe,

And we will fight you

To breathe

To our last breath,

For we are the most

Powerful humans

And you are just a

Circle of stones

Which we the humans

Named

STONEHENGE.

CHAPTER FIVE:

AUNT MARINDA

"Hidden within
A mirror
Is your soul.
Your body remains
In front of the mirror.
Yet then,
Where are you
For is the
Mirror you
Controlled by the
Physical you?"

Nightfall came sooner than we had anticipated. The sky above our roof was pink and beautiful. In normal situations, I love the countryside of Greater London and the surrounding areas.

Alice was sleeping like a baby. For some reason, the woman in front of us had attracted us to her. Like a magnet, she pulled all of us as we were glued onto her. Uncle Kees stayed in her room and refused to let her go. Griet and Rietje slept next to her in the same bed as if they were the best of friends. I worried what it was about the woman that had even melted my rough and tough heart.

I wondered who she was. She screamed at us and almost sent us away. Why did she say she was Mrs. Avyaan when he never married? I called the Vrederic Hospital London to get some explanation on the Dr. Avyaan we had visited. To my surprise, he answered the phone. He refused to talk but sent a text message saying, "Can't talk. Hope you all settled in safely. Will be there ASAP."

Mama has a way of making even rundown houses into a home. I didn't have the courage to ask Mama if she cooked from old, canned vegetables or hoped maybe my baby niece had given mysterious foods from her basket of bread.

Mama had food delivered and set on the very broken table. I thought it was Mama's home and not that we were all unwanted guests at the home of a woman who was absolutely lying about her identity. Papa was sitting on a very old recliner which I knew was going to collapse and hurt him on the way. Yet he made it seem so comfortable. I wondered if Mama was all right.

I saw my brothers stare at me as Andries said, "She did it on her own. I promise you. We had no idea. During the time you were busy at the hospital trying to heal Alice, some guys delivered the food and left the bags on the porch. They ran away so fast that I thought they saw a ghost when Mama walked outside and asked them why they were so late. They were in front of the cottage walking around as if it was invisible and they couldn't see it. We thought it was strange how they screamed and ran so fast. I know people fear Kasteel Vrederic, but this cottage too? The guys were just walking around and saying, 'Why on Earth would someone give this creepy place as an address to deliver food?'"

I laughed out loud as Mama heard and saw me. I kissed my mother and was proud of her. She tried to give everyone as much as she could. I knew she must have more intuitions she wasn't sharing. I wouldn't probe her as she would share at her own time and place. Mama never tries to

ANN MARIE RUBY

attract attention to herself. She is the most giving person in this world, but she will share only when she knows for a fact what her dreams had shown her is accurate. I only wondered why the delivery guys ran and feared Mama.

After Mama overheard us, she said, "Dear Andries, if you and Antonius had been awake to see everything, you would have had the answer. Not everything is as they seem. Maybe all of this is an illusion. We have our own mind and God-given knowledge to detach ourselves from reality and illusions. Until we can differentiate, we do what boys?"

My brothers and I knew the answer as we all screamed and told her together, "When in confusion, take a break and wait it out."

Papa nodded his head toward Uncle Kees who still sat on the same bed as Alice. He held on to her hands and kept repeating the same phrase.

He again very quietly said, "Who are you? What if even God is now upset at us? Oh my God, was it a sin to fall for a dead person at the beginning? Is that why I have been punished? What happens if we get separated forever? Will you still love me from where you are? I will keep on asking, who you are, as I feel my beloved's breath and smells around you. Why?"

122

We listened to Uncle Kees's words without breathing, in fear we would miss what he said. There were no sounds and no movements. No one spoke. I tried to see Mama and Papa's reaction. I tried to ask Papa with my eyes, what was happening. Andries kept winking as did Antonius toward Papa.

Andries said, "Oh my God, is Uncle Kees cheating on Aunt Marinda? Hmm Uncle Kees, I'm telling when we do find out where Aunt Marinda is."

Andries, Antonius, and I knew what was coming next. Andries got slapped on his back by Mama as did Antonius and I. We never asked anymore why we all got punished when one of us did something stupid. Antonius and I looked at Andries in a way he knew we were upset at him, yet no one said anything.

Papa sat down as he said, "I am lost and don't know what's happening. As an artist, this house is strange. I feel like the artist who drew this home forgot to place a heart inside of this home. This house looks like a crypt, not a house."

Antonius walked with his eyes closed for a while. As a blind artist, his sixth sense had always guided him in life. He walked straight to Mama. He then opened his eyes and kept eye contact with Mama for a while.

Antonius then said, "Big Mama, you were my eyes when I was blind. You blindfolded yourself for me and guided me through my darkness. It's not my sixth sense that guided me but you my mother was and shall always be my sixth sense, my guide. What's going on Big Mama?"

My two brothers are biologically my cousins who became orphans when their parents had died in a car accident. Mama and Papa adopted them and told them in this house they had three sons, not adopted but just sons. Mama asked them to call her and Papa, Big Mama and Big Papa, so they always knew and honored their parents and never forgot them.

Mama held Antonius on his shoulders as she always did because he was born blind. She still does the same gestures even after he got his sight back.

She said, "My son, always visit things through your inner eye. We entered a house that is made of stones. It was covered in weeds and vines. On top of the house was standing Incubus the demon. Ask yourself, where are we? I didn't go shopping but things appeared when I needed them. The food, however, I ordered and by the actions of the delivery guys, I would have thought they walked into a graveyard not a cottage."

Papa watched Mama for a long time as he nodded his head. Somehow, they spoke with one another without saying anything. I realized something very scary was going on in here. I asked the person who had the answers to all of this.

I softly and calmly whispered to a young child who was sitting on the couch next to Papa, "Theunis, what is going on? Where are we? Do you have the answers, or do we need to call him again?"

Theunis, the child, held on to Papa and was having a hard time understanding us. I wondered if we were in a tunnel of some kind where even Theunis couldn't speak. Griet walked over to me and touched my sleeves.

I picked her up in my arms as she said, "Papa Jacobus, we entered a pyramid. This is not a house but a pyramid that was hidden away. It's Aunt Marinda's pyramid. She was buried here alive. Theunis has a hard time doing anything in coffins. He feels like he gets imprisoned."

I realized even when Theunis had entered the coffin to be with Griet in the sixteenth century, I had opened the coffin which allowed Theunis to keep himself and Griet in spirit form until Rietje passed away. So many lessons are hidden within the Kasteel Vrederic library, I have to go back and read all of the diaries again to completely understand everything.

I told Mama, "I am confused and lost. Mama, please help."

She sat next to Papa and said, "I believe if my dreams are to be a guide, then we entered a hidden pyramid. Instead of a sarcophagus, it's like a small hut because the woman they tried to bury alive had immortality."

Mama pointed toward Margriete for something. She knew and immediately got Mama a cup of tea. Tara Bella got Papa one cup, as Katelijne gave the rest of the adults fresh cups of tea and she poured the children milk and honey.

Mama sipped her tea and then continued, "You can't murder immortal beings, but you can imprison them by trapping them inside a coffin, a house, or something airtight. Someone can set them free by taking the bodies out into the open air without knowing who they are taking out was buried alive. That's why Theunis has a hard time being inside of coffins or even pyramids."

Wondrously the diary in Uncle Kees's hands started to glow. In the diary, there was a mirror where we could see Aunt Marinda appear. The light was shining so brightly that everyone had to close their eyes. A fragment of a woman appeared in the light. Aunt Marinda walked out of the mirror and dusted something off herself.

She smiled at Uncle Kees and said, "As a time traveler, I had traveled time to be with all of you when you all needed me. I still can travel time through my dreams. Yes, dead people or half dead people too have dreams. This body you see is just a vehicle we the living use to travel with."

Uncle Kees was watching Aunt Marinda's light form as we all saw teardrops fall silently. No words were uttered nor were heard. There in front of us stood a very elegant white woman with blond hair and blue eyes. She watched Uncle Kees, the tall bronze man with long braids guarding her.

He said, "For thousands of years, I had lingered for you. I guarded you as the stars in the high skies. I became flowers upon Earth to make sure you always have fresh flowers around if you ever had opened your eyes. My beloved, why is it I feel you within the body of this Earthly woman who looks nothing like you?"

There in bed, was sleeping a woman who had fair skin, brown hair, and brown eyes. She looked so frail. I didn't know who was who, and who was lifeless, the light form in front of us, or the woman in bed.

I saw my daughter Rietje walk in between the light form and the frail woman in bed, saying in her childlike voice, "Aunt Marinda, I am tired. I want bread and butter and maybe some milk."

She then said with more authority, "Your baby Rietje is hungry please."

The woman in the bed rushed to sit up. She was very wobbly and could barely get up. She got out of bed, stood up, and tried to open her eyes. She walked toward a wall where there was a mirror.

In front of the mirror, she said, "I must travel time. Help me Theunis, please. Rietje is hungry. I must travel time and help her. I must rush and save her. She is your child and now the daughter of my beloved Jacobus. I must help."

It was so confusing as I wondered then who was the woman in the diary. In Uncle Kees's diary was hidden a mirror which was buried with Uncle Kees. Who was the woman inside of that mirror if Aunt Marinda was here and her mirror too was here buried with her?

The woman in the mirror which was shining in amber gold screamed now and said, "Jacobus, it's me! I am your aunt! Don't be fooled by her. She is that woman, that horror woman, that demoness. I am your aunt. I am the woman in the mirror."

I wondered what was going on. How could there be two mirrors and two women claiming to be Aunt Marinda?

Who was the real one? Why would Uncle Kees hold on to the hands of the woman who had screamed at us and said she was Mrs. Alice Avyaan?

Uncle Kees got up and without letting go of the woman who called herself Alice, asked, "In life or in?"

We saw the frail woman pause and reply, "Or in death."

Then Uncle Kees asked her, "For you, I shall become?"

The frail woman again replied, "Ashes to ashes, dust to dust."

Pin-drop silence overtook the small cottage of death where a body was buried alive. Neither the cottage nor the body could be seen or felt as if they didn't even exist.

Uncle Kees somehow lit a fire with his hands. I never knew nor realized Uncle Kees too had his own powers as he too was buried in a sarcophagus within a pyramid.

He lit the fire and asked, "If I burn my beloved in a fire?"

The frail woman walked toward the fire that was now burning in the living room of the small cottage, and said, "I will burn with you and become ashes with you, to only be with you."

I saw the woman who had walked out of the mirror walk backward. She looked just like Aunt Marinda did in the sixteenth century, but she was different. She changed her face as the fire was getting bigger. She screamed and shouted out loud.

She yelled, "It's your fault Incubus! You tricked me into this. You told me to hide in this diary and they will all assume I'm Marinda. You said they will foolishly set me free. It's Kees and his foolish love story! The 'in life or in death' phrase said by lovers are set free by God who resides above in Heaven and whom even we the demons can't ever fight. You stupid fool! I will never burn myself or die for you, or anyone. Love my foot you psycho!"

She was now changing, and her face became old and decaying like an old witch. She howled as if she was in pain. At the same time, I saw Aunt Marinda become rejuvenated and herself with blonde hair and blue eyes.

Succubus, whose real name in this life was Alice, screamed in pain. It was like a windstorm had come and the mirror that was hidden in Aunt Marinda's diary by apparently Succubus herself, disappeared as we were then standing in an open area near the Stonehenge. There were no signs of the stone cottage.

In front of us was standing Incubus the demon. He was laughing like a monster and looked nasty. I don't know why anyone would even fall for him as his true form was nothing like our Theunis.

Incubus then said, "My name is Daemon. I am an evil spirit who has been roaming around from, well you can say the beginning of time. People know me as Incubus as there are a lot of demons like me who are all called Incubus. My wife Alice is also known as Succubus as demonesses like her are all called Succubus. Theunis is now the King of all demons, so I must also comply to his rules and as promised, I will help you but please remember, I am evil. Theunis is good, and at times it will be good against bad, but I will not fight my own son."

He was just standing there, so proud of himself. He wanted to say much more but was fighting with himself not to say anything.

Then, he said, "Demons engage in sex within themselves. If they do happen to engage with humans, they sire half demons. The sired children usually become mentally unstable. Rarely they are normal and just have extra powers. Theunis is an example of a very rare human with extra powers."

As Daemon walked around without making any sound, he saw his son Theunis, laughed, and said, "She is a demoness, yet I always wondered why she never had any feelings for you, her only son. I realize she is no different than humans who dump their children and don't care. Just as humans have good, we the demons have within us some good and some very bad. Fight her with all the good you have as she will fight you with all her evil deeds."

Like a maze in a desert, we were all standing in an open area. I saw there were graves around us. A headstone we bumped into read, "Daemon the Incubus. Born into evil as even my biological humans used to give birth to me were all evil. Be good and fight evil with good for the only thing feared by all evil is good."

Suddenly Mama started to cry and said, "I don't feel for you even if you tried to be good. Maybe that's just the mother inside of my body, but evil is just a choice, and you chose to be one."

Daemon laughed for a while and as he was going further and further away, he whispered, "Like your Aunt Marinda never let any evil enter her life, not even in her dreams. You too are a woman who never allowed any demons to enter your life or dreams. Your good deeds are feared by even the worst and most powerful demons. As I said, evil is defeated by good."

Daemon was again laughing like he lost his mind. I didn't know if we should believe anything he said or just run and hide. Where do we hide from demons who are always one step ahead of us? Maybe we should do as Mama said and wait it out.

Daemon then spoke again, "I salute you both for being like this. Never change. I will for this one reason always help and be there for you both. Stay safe Marinda as now you have a human body to live your life with your beloved. The evil woman in the mirror will try to hunt you down. Stay aware and look all around you before you trust anyone. Yes, I found out where she had hidden you Marinda, so I led all your family members here. She had the mirror hidden inside of your diary Kees to always stay one step ahead of you. She buried your physical body, Marinda, here in a grave where once had stood a hut built by the famous sixteenth-century merchant Johannes van Vrederic. That is why you were safe."

Thunder roared in the skies above us. We knew it was Alice the Succubus. She would not rest until she got her ways.

We all heard her screech and declare war upon us as she said, "I will never rest until I can have you as my own, Kees. I will fight till the end. You might call me crazy, but this is my unguarded unrequited love for you, Kees. I will have you even if that's what will make me mortal, and I must give up my immortality. I am coming for you Marinda, just wait and see."

We heard shrieks of anger all around us like a banshee. The screeching sound hurt everyone's ears. The children were crying as I saw Theunis place his hands up and the sounds faded.

Then we heard her say, "Theunis, I will not let you or your beloved Kasteel Vrederic family members rest or live in peace, as it's you who had me vanquished from my own world. You and your good deeds are my enemies eternally, and they belong under my feet. I will come for every single one of your family members even if that's the last thing I do. Daemon, I will never forgive you, nor will I let you go!"

I heard Daemon the Incubus laugh again as I wondered if he thought everything in life was fun and games for him. They were both immortal, so they didn't fear end of times or the apocalypse. So, they just lived and played their lives like games.

Daemon the Incubus kept on laughing as he said to Alice the Succubus, "Game on, sweetheart."

Aunt Marinda was very fragile as she observed all of us and for the first time in centuries, I saw my favorite aunt who had always guarded my family and me throughout time. I saw her and knew for the first time she looked scared. I also realized true love never faded as even when no one knew, Uncle Kees knew the fragile rude woman was actually his beloved Marinda.

I told my Aunt Marinda, "Dear beloved aunt, this nephew of yours will always guard you within my chest. You are protected and forever safe within the shelters of my heart. Never shall I let you go ever again. This is my vow, a vow from an honorable nephew."

The dark night greeted us with a starless night. We drove our camper back to London where I knew waited for us, Dr. Avyaan. I wondered what the mystery behind Dr. Avyaan was. Right now, however, we wanted to listen to a love story that was lost from the pages of this world, the immortal love story of Kees and Marinda.

Our camper moved toward London as we all remained quiet during the two-hour drive. Never in my life did a short drive like this one appear so long. Mama sat next to Papa while he drove like a calm and persistent pilot. The children were all awake and I had no heart to ask them to try to nap.

We didn't know what laid ahead of us, but I knew we would all be ready. The children had seen and gone through more than any children on Earth would ever go through. Everyone in the camper enjoyed the quiet drive and at times wanted this ride to never end. Aunt Marinda sat next to the children as did Uncle Kees.

Theunis was talking with Aunt Marinda as he asked her, "How long will you protect this family? Also, where is the mirror that was in the house?"

Aunt Marinda got worried, and she tried to think in her mind.

She saw Griet and asked her, "I don't know where the mirror is that was on the wall, but I will protect you all eternally, in life or even after death."

Little Griet smiled and hugged Aunt Marinda as did Little Rietje. Mama was smiling at the children as she saw Alexander, our young warrior, thinking as if he too was worried.

Mama said, "Never fear for Mama here. I broke the mirror before I came, or before the house disappeared. I remembered Aunt Marinda had told me through one of her time-traveling journeys, the way to set a person imprisoned within a mirror free is to just break it. The seven years of bad luck must have been placed by demons who wanted to keep souls as prisoners."

Aunt Marinda laughed out loud and got up and hugged Mama.

She said, "I have no fear as I have my family here. Yes, it's true the seven years of bad luck was the only way demons could control humans. Fear is the only way to control the mind of an innocent. So, never fear for the end of all miseries are just ahead of you, all the fearless warriors."

I watched my favorite aunt, and I felt like a big burden had been lifted. Maybe we would be able to unite the lovers who had been waiting to be united for centuries. Now before we could go forward anymore, we all demanded we needed to hear the love story of Kees and Marinda.

I told everyone, "Now, come on everyone, let's all listen to the immortal love story that began centuries ago. The lovers have given all of us our love stories as Aunt Marinda helped unite us all throughout time."

Our whole family checked into a hotel near the Vrederic Hospital London. We got a family quarter which had a huge family room with a huge stone fireplace. We decided to sleep together in the family room. We told the children it was because we would be camping. I wondered if we tried to comfort the brave children or make sure we all stayed safe together. We had asked Aunt Marinda and Uncle Kees to take the one bedroom that was decorated like a honeymoon suite. As we settled for the night in the family room, we all said at once, "We want to listen to the eternal love story from Aunt Marinda."

AUNT MARINDA

Love stories

You helped create

For all the

Family members

Of your beloved

Twin flame.

Without any gratitude,

From all the people

You had helped,

Your given promise

Never did break apart

Throughout

Life and even

Within death.

You kept your given oath.

To love

And to be loved,

You taught

Through your

Time-traveling

Adventures.

Eternally faithful,

Forever loyal,

Your love remained

With all those

You have touched,

With your guidance, and

With your love.

Within your protection,

You have kept

All your beloved

Family members.

Dear beloved,

Today we the beloved

Give you our oath,

And promise.

We shall be there for you,

Visibly,

Invisibly,

Like the hands

Of blessings.

We shall all cover you,

Protect you, and

Always make sure this time

In this life,

It is not just

Our love stories,

But your immortal

Love story

Too finds its path

And makes a bridge

Of union

Between you,

And your beloved.

We shall all draw

The bridge of union

For your beloved Kees,

And his beloved Marinda.

Our beloved,

And ever-loving,

Most adored,

Much treasured,

Eternally prized,

Everyone's favored,

AUNT MARINDA.

CHAPTER SIX:

KEES AND MARINDA VAN VREDERIC

"*Two separate bodies,*
Two separate souls,
And
Two separate
Individuals created
One love story."

The lifeless body of a woman arrived at Kasteel Vrederic in the early sixteenth century. The great merchant Johannes van Vrederic received the coffin of this unknown woman. I was watching a great love story being born through the eyes of the greatest psychic, the time traveler of Kasteel Vrederic.

Aunt Marinda wrote her immortal story in her diary and gave me her famous diary. As I held on to the book, it became a mirror, a television screen where we all saw a movie being played. Neither could we join the cast, nor could we interfere as this story took place centuries ago and was forever immortal in the past. A time traveler, however, could go back in time or journey to the future with restricted rules she had to follow. We knew Aunt Marinda never helped herself as she could not, but she tried to save all of us throughout the centuries. This was a time traveler's diary.

We viewed on the screen a love story that never came to fruition. I saw Papa in his sixteenth-century form as Johannes van Vrederic, a noble and arrogant merchant, accept the coffin.

He said to the soldiers, "All of you can leave. I will have her buried in my family grounds. She is my sister that I never had."

All the cavalry soldiers, carriages, war horses, and packhorses that brought the coffin left. Papa bent down and cried on top of the coffin. I worried why he was crying as I knew my father in that lifetime was known as a cold-hearted person.

He then said to the coffin, "You promised to be here with Jacobus forever. I can't raise him alone. He is motherless, and I know I had lost myself when my beloved wife passed away. Please tell me what I am to do. You are the only one who knows I am ill. I don't know if I will have all the memories of today to tell everyone tomorrow."

A light appeared from behind Papa, and I saw Aunt Marinda standing like a lighted spirit angel.

She smiled and said, "My love story too had ended as I don't know where he is. Yet he lives with our memories. My life's purpose will be to guard and protect Jacobus as I promised in life, I would do it even after death. My love story will have to wait centuries as does yours Johannes. Some love stories take centuries and that's good because our story continues as does our everlasting love."

Papa seemed tired and frail while he opened the gate that evening as the sun was setting behind Kasteel Vrederic. He invited a warrior inside the castle. Uncle Kees entered Kasteel Vrederic. I wondered why Uncle Kees had said he never placed his feet inside of Kasteel Vrederic in his lifetime. Also, why was Aunt Marinda dead inside of a coffin saying her love story ended before it had a chance?

Uncle Kees said, "I brought the coffin to you as you asked me to do so. I don't know why I feel like I know you and the dead woman, yet all I can remember is that a woman who called herself Succubus had tried to kill her and eventually did. She said she would burn her on the stakes over the centuries. Succubus also threatened to kill all of your family members. I just don't know how I'm involved in this whole thing. Do I know the woman in the coffin? Are you in some way related to me? I only remember someone had hurt me and took me as a prisoner."

Papa surveyed Uncle Kees and it was so obvious he had no clue as to who Uncle Kees was or who Succubus was. I knew he knew something in his mind, but his memories failed him. He was trying to fight but was lost inside of himself. My father was suffering from the shock of losing his wife from which he never recovered. He tried to hide from everyone.

He went closer to Uncle Kees and tried to see something in his eyes. He stood there like a lost person. As a doctor, I saw he had early symptoms of dementia and was trying to gather his thoughts but could not comprehend why he couldn't remember everything or get his thoughts together.

I realized he would pretend to know everything and everyone around him for years, as no one would catch on that he just couldn't remember them or things. Everyone had said he was a very hot-tempered and unkind person. I didn't know why even I couldn't catch on to his illness but thought he was just very introverted and liked to keep things to himself.

Papa said, "I swear I feel like you could be my brother, but I'm lost in my own mind. It's a horrifying thing when you lose your mind. Marinda was my healer. She promised to take care of my baby boy and me. She said she would heal me, and I would forget my wife and all the pain of losing her. I want to forget her so much that I have basically erased my whole life."

I saw Papa wander off in his own mind for a while, then he said, "Why would she get involved with a demoness called Succubus and die? I needed her. She shouldn't have gotten herself involved in things that would take her away from us. I miss her."

Uncle Kees watched my father, and he laughed out loud. He was probably thinking how selfish are the rich as they only think of themselves. A woman just died and you are worried about your son and yourself.

Papa, however, didn't care about wealth or name. He was trying to remember his day-to-day life. Somehow, he was living the same day over and over. He knew he had a baby boy. He missed his dead wife, and he knew Aunt Marinda and Bertelmeeus. He tried to take everything in and just fainted. Bertelmeeus rushed out from somewhere and entered the room. He had other helpers take Papa. Bertelmeeus had a small baby in his arms, and I knew the child was myself in the sixteenth century.

Bertelmeeus placed the baby in a small day crib as he opened the coffin. I saw a lighted figure jump out and come and take me in her arms. No one saw her but Bertelmeeus. He smiled and cried at the same time. Papa was sent to bed as Uncle Kees took the coffin that was to be interred in our family crypt. I knew this was before I started the *Evermore Beloved* garden, our ancestral burial ground.

The woman smiled and stayed behind. A mirror appeared out of the coffin. Uncle Kees saw the mirror and I watched tears spill from his eyes. Even though Uncle Kees was under a spell of some kind where someone erased his memories, his love was so strong that he still knew and loved his beloved Marinda.

His wife was accused of being a witch. She was bewitched and placed in a coffin. No one can erase or separate twin flames. It's like twin flames live in life and even in death with one another's eternal wedded ties.

With a lot of sadness, I saw a twin flame kiss the dead woman as he lost the battle of control to his own tears. The tears failed him as they fell upon the dead woman. As the teardrops touched the dead woman, like magic, a glistening rose began to bloom above her chest.

He said to Bertelmeeus, "She is so beautiful. I feel like I knew her. She was with me and said something about herself, but I can't remember anything. Even though I promised to be with her eternally, I wonder how a black man like me could marry a white woman. No one said I couldn't love her in my heart. Why is it something inside of my heart beats and will stop beating only for her? Please don't tell anyone I kissed a dead woman. Is she really dead? She seems to be alive and warm to the touch."

That's when I saw Aunt Marinda tell Bertelmeeus, "You can see me right? I was promised to have eternal life if I was going to be hung at the gallows or burned on the stakes by false accusations. I am a time traveler, and I can stay alive through time traveling until my husband and Jacobus come back for me. I will wait for everyone by the

Stonehenge where I have been interred in a stone hut. Yes, Johannes will keep me safe there in the stone hut he had bought only for me near the Stonehenge. It's like I will be near the demoness, but she won't be able to harm me. She will think she hid me there."

Uncle Kees kept saying, "I love you my wife and I promise I will come back for you."

As he was fainting on top of the coffin, he said, "Take care of my nephew Jacobus. He is the only bloodline we will have left. Jacobus will have a daughter through whom our family will all be reunited."

Bertelmeeus walked over and carried the baby in his arms as he asked the glowing figure, "Marinda, how did all of this happen? Why did you marry a black man when society discourages interracial marriages? For whom have you passed away?"

Aunt Marinda became more like a normal human rather than a lighted figure, and she walked around and took the baby from Bertelmeeus as she kissed the baby and said, "For you my beloved nephew, I live and so does your Uncle Kees. From your lineage, we will all come back. Remember my love for you is eternal with or without my heartbeats as my heart beats your name."

Aunt Marinda kissed Bertelmeeus on the cheek as she was somehow related to him too. Aside from Papa, Bertelmeeus was the only person I had in that time as a family member who ever loved me like a son.

Aunt Marinda then said, "I love him Bertelmeeus more than my own heartbeats. He loves me more than his own, yet destiny had a demoness who too wants my husband for herself. She will fight until the world ends to have him or make sure I never have him. Bertelmeeus, never tell this to anyone unless Jacobus returns in another time and place. Know my husband Kees van Vrederic is Johannes van Vrederic's twin brother. Their mother was black."

She then disappeared but left a diary with Bertelmeeus. He picked up the diary and placed the diary in the coat pockets of Uncle Kees who was walking in a daze as if he was in a desert and everything to him was just a mirage. He kept saying something, but we couldn't understand the words.

Anyone in this world or beyond who has ever fallen in love would all realize his words were the agonies and painful cries of a beloved. We all saw in the video playing in front of us, a lover's painful cries and his quiet soundless tears were writing a love story that was cursed by someone whose curses should never even be. This immortal love story had to wait as even though the love story was immortal, these two fighting for their beloveds were somewhat mortal.

One was a time traveler and the other was buried in a sarcophagus. They didn't die, but they stayed alive for one another. I knew they kept each other alive throughout time and tide. They agreed they would wait until the end of time, if needed, to have any happily ever after. They didn't cry or worry about time as their love was eternal even though their time together was not.

Bertelmeeus said, "I don't want to read any personal diaries. You will know what to do with it. Wake up and please take the diary to safety. Keep the diary with you forever as that's what Marinda would have wanted you to do. We will have her interred in the family crypt if that's your wish. Or we can have her buried somewhere safe as that's what Johannes would want."

Papa came downstairs, walked to the open courtyard in front of Kasteel Vrederic, and said, "This castle has so many secrets hidden within its walls. One is I know Marinda won't ever die as she is a time traveler. I don't know how but she will be back. Who was that person who came with the coffin? I am assuming he was her beloved. I don't know how but if he comes back tell him I will have her body safely secured for him until she is ready to return. That's what I saw in my dreams just now. It was a strange dream as I saw I must have her buried at one of my private cottages far away from Naarden, near London and the Stonehenge."

Bertelmeeus walked outside as he was trying to figure out the gibberish words that were coming out of my father's mouth. I realized Papa knew more than he was saying but his memories were impacted by the loss of Mama.

Aunt Marinda joined them outside and said, "My love story will begin again as you let my husband Kees take my diary which has a mirror inside of it. He forgot all about me and that's what Succubus had wanted him to do. He will remember me in death or in life for you can never separate twin flames. Twin flames rise together in life after life, in life or in death, together forever. Even though Succubus will try to hide her mirror and change mine, I will be in the cottage waiting for her."

Aunt Marinda walked closer to Papa as a confused Papa surveyed her for a while. She held his hands and gave him a hug.

She said, "Johannes, you don't know but he is related to you through blood. You will not prove this truth in this life but will in another time and at the same place within the same courtyard of Kasteel Vrederic. You will unite with your beloved brother, and I too will come and join you and my beloved nephew Jacobus in his reincarnated form."

Papa said, "Did you know my beloved wife was a Hindu? She was an Indian woman who was burned to ashes because she married me, a white man. I don't want to live Marinda for I just don't know how to go on without her."

Aunt Marinda's spirit form remained with Papa and she cried for him. I wondered what about her love story which was lost in the lost papers of history? It was not written nor known by anyone else but the two beloveds.

Aunt Marinda then told Papa, "Listen to my words carefully. This castle must remain in the family because this is where all the future generations will find safety and security. This house and the family members will always have me anywhere or anytime if they are ever in trouble or when they need me. I will guide them physically or as a spirit. Even death can't keep a time traveler like me away from my beloved's family members."

Papa looked at her confusedly for a while, then he just smiled without saying anything.

Bertelmeeus watched both and said, "Marinda please write everything down in your diary. Johannes won't remember anything in the morning. He knows you are like a sister to him, but he won't remember you have passed away.

He won't remember anything about the person who brought the coffin which had your body inside. Maybe you can still come and visit Jacobus and me without telling anyone you are dead. Everyone will know you are a time traveler or that you are a psychic."

I watched Bertelmeeus take the baby inside with him as a diary was being written with a golden pen on a mirror. The diary was given to Kees as he walked out with the diary in his hands. He placed the mirror inside of his shirt inside the jacket he was wearing.

I saw as he stepped outside, he opened the coffin and said, "Please tell me what to do. You are safe here. I must separate from you, so she never takes your body away from me. I couldn't have you in life and now even in death I can't have you. You have left this Earth, so how will we unite? Take me with you. Please help me keep your memories alive within my chest. I have nothing but your memories, and that too she has attacked. I am forgetting everything, even our love story."

I saw Aunt Marinda's ghost shine within the courtyard of Kasteel Vrederic. No one witnessed the tears of a broken man who had lost everything in his life. How could he tell everyone a demoness had separated them because she wanted Kees for herself. She didn't hesitate to murder her own Aunt Marinda because she wanted her aunt's husband. In the sixteenth century, Succubus was related to Aunt Marinda by blood.

Like a nightmare, I saw Succubus standing outside of the castle as she said, "Oh Kees, now I will take you to the Sahara Desert where you will be buried in a sarcophagus. Your beloved wife, even if she tries to travel time, will never find you. This family will be childless, and no one will ever come back or be reincarnated from this castle. I will have sex with you as soon as you give me permission to do so. You won't even know I am not your Marinda, I promise you. So, you will be only mine. Then, I will dump you. Your Marinda can just rot like trash."

Without any notice, from somewhere Papa walked outside and said to Succubus directly, "You the ugly woman standing outside of my gate, how dare you scream in front of my home. This is a family home not a brothel for women like you. How dare you curse this home to be childless. Leave!"

Papa held his head up high and had his eyes locked to Succubus directly without any fear and said, "I am a gentleman who has lost his wife. With her memories in my inner soul, I curse you. I believe in reincarnation, and I promise Heaven above will bring my beloved and me back as this family will continue. I'm not scared of any evil demon or human as I am a good man. In a war of good and bad, good is always victorious."

Papa walked to the courtyard and touched the walls of our home. He was in his mind praying or asked the home to give him strength.

Then he said to the evil woman, "I promise you, this family will have children and that too shall be your gift to us. As members of this home, we will make sure you and your lovers are cursed and shall be hated by your own child. May your own son ruin you for tormenting Marinda and my people and the people who are helping with the coffin."

Papa walked around the castle grounds as he hounded the demoness. He looked really tired. Even though his memories were failing him, he tried to keep his own stand.

Papa then shouted loudly unlike himself, "May my curses cross time and tide and even in my reincarnated form, may my curses hold you a prisoner! For reasons I don't know, I want you to be the prisoner in a mirror! Yes, you Succubus or demoness threatening my sister shall be the woman in the mirror. You will never be real. I pray we get a gift from you and have a real woman like my dead wife, or maybe someone similar to her, in the mirror who shall protect our home eternally."

Papa had the courage to curse the evil woman who had begun her torturing tormenting war with our family. I figured he remembered he had to take care of Aunt Marinda, his beloved friend he considered his sister. It was not known to him at the time that she was his sister-in-law.

Aunt Marinda watched all of this as we saw the demoness disappear with Uncle Kees. Although Aunt Marinda's body was left behind, the demoness took something from Aunt Marinda's coffin.

Succubus laughed and said, "You all will never be born to even regret anything."

I realized she took Aunt Marinda's mirror. In the present time, somehow through a mirror from our hotel room, we had entered the courtyard of Kasteel Vrederic during the sixteenth century. As we were witnessing the past incidents, no one else other than Aunt Marinda could see us. Miraculously we were all still viewing the events taking course in the same courtyard of our home, separated by us through time.

Aunt Marinda saw us, and she smiled at us from the past. As she saw my reincarnated form and she saw Papa's reincarnated form, she smiled and blew kisses to us from the past. She then asked Bertelmeeus in the sixteenth century to give her the baby.

She kissed the baby's head and his cheeks, and she said, "Eternally and evermore, I shall love you. This is my vow from the beyond my baby nephew. I will help raise you and your family members and keep all of you safe, not because I need you but because I love you all with my mind, body, and soul. Your Papa, even in his lost world, has kept my honor and without any fear cursed the demoness who ruined my life. For the curse from an innocent, your family which is my family will unite again in another time. She stole one mirror which she will travel time through, yet never fear for I have more. There will be a woman who will come. Her sketch will appear on the mirror. Only when her soul is set free through death, will she be able to travel from one life to another, and be the saving grace of Kasteel Vrederic."

Everyone in the family room of the hotel had tears rolling down their cheeks. Then, the video continued and in pin-drop silence, we all watched. I again wondered where this mirror with the sketch was. Why did I feel like I had seen it so many times but couldn't remember or place my fingers to it.

In the skies on top of Kasteel Vrederic, I saw written, "Some love stories are written with tears and these tears will make the love stories eternal. Water erases everything except tears pouring from a beloved's eyes become the elixir of life. These love stories and the beholders of these stories will live on eternally even though their bodies might not. Love never dies, not in separation nor in death. True love and true lovers will reunite throughout time. I will be back, through life or even from beyond death, as my beloved will live on through our love story. This elixir that has poured from my eyes will be stored in this home called Kasteel Vrederic. It will wait for you all as you will need it sometime in the future."

The mirror was shining light at the rooftop of Kasteel Vrederic where I knew in the future had the lighthouse installed. I saw my family members were crying as tears fell without any restrictions. Papa saw the past life's events and just held Mama in his arms. He held his brother Kees and gave him a hug.

Papa said, "With or without memories, we will never be separated as we are all the family of Kasteel Vrederic. In this lifetime, I promise I will avenge all the harm Succubus caused to my family members. The love stories in our homes are eternal. Within our home, all love stories will end in happily ever after even if it takes more than one life to make it happen."

I was speechless even though normally, words come to me easily when I must write them or say them in my mind, or at least medical words. I have always found myself lost with words when I felt more emotions than my soul could take. The woman who had always been there for me, had become more than anything in this world to me. My love for Aunt Marinda is eternal. It always has been eternal, without even knowing any of her sacrifices or her love story.

I only said, "Eternal vows from the beyond I take as I will cross life or death to make sure the holy union of this blessed couple, I love more than I could ever express in words, shall be. This couple, my family is blessed to have and know as the only two who to this day carry the surname of our blessed home Kasteel Vrederic, also known to this world as Kees van Vrederic and Marinda van Vrederic.

With the end of each chapter, I included a poem for all of you to understand my family's diary. Yet in this chapter I have included a poem written by Aunt Marinda and Uncle Kees during their marriage in the sixteenth century.

KEES AND
MARINDA VAN VREDERIC

Love lives on

Beyond time,

Beyond the stars,

Beyond the Earth

As love stories

Are written

With

The sacrifices

Of two lovers.

What about

When twin flames

Are separated,

Are forced to forget

One another, and

Are kept separated

By time and tide?

Does love end

When the tides wash away?

Does love fade

When sandcastles

Are washed away?

What happens when the

Heart beats no more?

Is it then the

Beloved's beatless

Hearts

Stop loving

And stop feeling

For one another?

Or does

Love live on

Beyond time,

Beyond heartbeats, and

Beyond bodies becoming ashes?

True lovers,

The twin flames,

Are never separated

Even when the

Earthly bodies beat no more.

The twin flames

Rise from ashes

As mystical phoenixes

To only find

One another

Over and over again,

To say

To one another,

I love you today,

I shall love you tomorrow,

And eternally.

Even when

All but ends,

My love for

You and your love for me

Shall be eternally

Blessed.

Evermore be mine

As I shall be only yours.

This is and

Shall be our vow

As we are

True twin flames,

KEES AND

MARINDA VAN VREDERIC.

CHAPTER SEVEN:

THE INVISIBLE WAR

"Demons versus humans,
One instigates agony,
And
The other eliminates
The agony."

gony over what we can't control or see terrorized our family's inner peace. I knew at this time I needed to focus on the scientist inside of my body and then work from there. Everything that had started from Dr. Avyaan needed to be taken care of like solving a puzzle. Also, I reminded myself to talk to Dr. Smith.

The morning skies roared outside the hotel we reserved for the night. It felt like the world was preparing herself for a frightening paranormal war. The worst part was we saw in the news a lot of young women and men were being tortured. Dead bodies were appearing all around the world. The frightening part was, we all knew our enemies were invisible to us, yet we their prey were very visible to them. My only discomfort was how do we fight with what we cannot see, hear, or touch.

Mama was drinking her morning tea so calmly. I wanted some of her meditative harmony inside my soul.

She smiled and said, "All you can do is wait and let nature take over. You can't force things to be. Everything must take its course. I guess start with Dr. Hans Avyaan."

Aunt Marinda and Uncle Kees came over to us. Both of them slept on the recliners and did not try to have a quiet night together. I wanted to ask them if everything was all right, but I saw Mama tell me with her eyes not to say anything. I knew my mother's indications without her saying anything.

Uncle Kees wanted to say something, but Aunt Marinda said, "Not now Kees. I am fine and will be all right. Right now, we need to find your famous Dr. Avyaan who everyone for some weird reason had said was my husband. I don't ever recall knowing any Dr. Avyaan. I must have been under some kind of heavy weight."

Papa and my brothers walked in with the children who were planning to visit New York. For some reason, Dr. Ahmed had requested for my help. I knew I must make a quick visit and maybe I could also talk with Dr. Smith, the pyramidologist, who was also visiting New York City.

Aunt Marinda then asked Papa, "Erasmus could you take us to Kasteel Vrederic as soon as possible? That's the only place Succubus, or as I call her Alice, will not be able to enter. Also, I must share with you all something that happened last night."

Uncle Kees was inspecting all of us as we watched his wife speak. Mama gave everyone coffee and tea as they wished. We also had breakfast delivered to our apartment type quarter in the luxury hotel we were staying at. I appreciated how nice it felt to be in a normal apartment, not in the hut which Papa had originally bought. Yet this Papa had no clue about the hut or how it was a grave site, or when the cottage was sold and to whom.

Like my mother says, everything has its own answers and its own time and place of figuring out the answers. Papa watched Mama intensely for some reason. I knew he too knew more then they were sharing.

Aunt Marinda said with a sigh, "During the night, for some reason, I enter a mirror. Whenever Kees tries to touch me, I reenter the closest mirror. Kees needs to sleep in a closed closet or some place with light. So, the wedding night you all thought we were celebrating was a little strange."

Uncle Kees hugged his wife, kissed her head, and said, "It's not normal kisses or hugs. Marinda is shy and won't say or utter the words but it's like we can't have sex. If we try to get intimate, it's then she reenters a mirror. The hotel mirror is not what Marinda wants to be in. I hear there are a lot of infelicitous souls inside of it anyway."

Aunt Marinda laughed and took her morning tea. She sat down and saw all of us gazing at them with our own strange ways. We were numb and expressionless as we didn't know what was happening. It was always Aunt Marinda who guided us through all our troubles. I wondered who would guide her out of her troubled waters. I thought I would, somehow, someway.

Aunt Marinda laughed and said, "No worries, everyone. It was wonderful watching my husband all night from within the mirror. Our love is stronger than all obstacles combined. I enjoyed the night. Maybe it's when I can be there for all of you or anyone else if you all need me. Your Uncle Kees probably never told you all that he becomes lifeless at night. When he wakes up, he remembers everything. At night, Kees can see and hear everything but cannot move or do anything."

I stood up and thought to myself, was that a form of sleep paralysis? Yet all night, how? I would figure it out. There must be some simple physical reason. I saw my Margriete glance at me, and I knew a doctor's queries and worries at the same time.

Aunt Marinda laughed out loud and said, "He is not a vampire, nor am I a witch. It's because we have traveled time, like through the invisible staircases above the pyramids and yes, the Stonehenge too is a time-traveling tunnel. I must figure out why some part of our souls remained at other places causing this situation. Not to worry, we are here and will be here. We will enjoy our life together to the fullest for even to have a few more minutes together is a blessing."

Papa at that time stood up and kissed Aunt Marinda's cheek. He hugged her within his embrace. Everyone teared up and said nothing. Silence spoke louder than words.

He said, "I will have you two sent to the Netherlands. The rest of us will have to take a quick trip to New York as I promised Dr. Ahmed I would do so. I hope we can help catch Alice the Succubus as soon as possible or at least stop her from hurting another innocent life. She has gotten very mad and is hunting down as many innocent souls as she can."

Mama drank her second cup of tea as she got up and stretched. She wanted to say something but then decided not to say it. Instead, Mama walked away from the room. I knew when not to ask or question my mother, so I remained quiet.

I followed Papa who walked after Mama and asked him, "Papa what's going on? Why is Mama upset? She wanted to ask or say something but why did she just walk away?"

Papa was looking at me in a way, I knew there were others behind me. Obviously if I knew Mama was hiding something, my brothers knew she was hiding something too. They were just not behind me, but they were pushing me to go ahead and ask Mama. I thought, maybe not a bad idea. Let them ask. If anyone can do it, Andries can.

Antonius said, "Andries, go ask her. You are the baby and Mama never says no to you. So, go and just ask her what's going on."

Andries who could never keep anything inside ran after Mama. I told him in my mind, walk don't run but knew the words would go to deaf ears as when it's Mama we understood no reasoning.

Mama was sitting on a bench in the outdoor courtyard of our hotel suite. There was a fountain and arbors with climbing vines. Near the vines growing on the arbors were various colorful flower beds. It was like a honeymoon cabin. The whole atmosphere around the hotel was relaxing and calming. In a different situation, this would have been the perfect vacation.

We all stopped and froze in space as we saw Mama crying. It was not my brothers, nor I, but Aunt Marinda who followed all of us and spoke first.

She sat next to Mama and said, "Sweetheart I know you are a dream psychic, but you know I am a time-traveling psychic. I know what lays ahead of us. It's all good. The lesson of all time is good over evil. When and where there are good people standing, the evil will fall. It's that simple."

Aunt Marinda wiped off Mama's tears and they hugged as Mama said, "The message I got from my last night's dream was she will escape. How will we stop her if she gets away again? How many times do we need to fight her? Until we erase her from Earth, you two will never be able to consummate your marriage."

Uncle Kees laughed and hugged Mama as he said, "In love and joy, there are always tears and sorrows. True love and lovers, however, don't need anything but to have faith and patience. I know Marinda is mine throughout time, and she knows I am hers eternally. It matters not what happens, when it happens, or never does. We are together, so we have triumphed over all evil. My love story is complete as long as I can have my wife in my arms."

Andries was getting upset. He showed his feelings and stomped his feet like he used to do when he was a child. Antonius, even when he was blind, would also stomp his feet in anger when he wanted Mama. No one else could calm down his temper tantrums. I laughed to myself seeing both my brothers, the world-renowned pianist, and the famous painter, stomp their feet.

Mama got up and said, "Succubus will flee this time because she is a time traveler. We must catch and rescue the souls of the girls she is invading. Succubus's soul is imprisoned in the sixteenth century. She had imprisoned herself, so that she can be safe and do her invisible war. We can, as the inhabitants of this time, only protect the people she is trying to hunt down and those whose bodies she is using to hunt."

I understood why Mama was upset. We had an enemy who we could stop and remove from places and current times if we defeated the current physical body. We did that in Malibu, yet her original soul remained in the sixteenth century. As a time traveler, Succubus could travel and return so long as her original soul was intact in the sixteenth century. Throughout the centuries, she traveled time and entered different bodies. Succubus knew she would be safe if her original soul was safe.

We all knew our enemy was an invisible army. Succubus could travel time to escape her doom, but we her victims would not be able to catch her as we would always be limited to our time zone. No words were uttered. No questions were asked. My family members were all frozen as we knew our enemy always laid ahead of us and we were playing only to be safe and keep ourselves hidden.

Even though I thought demons don't come during the daylight hours, in bright daylight, we heard a laughing screech of a woman who sounded overjoyed and thrilled to be evil and victorious.

Mama got up and said, "How does she always know where we are? Or how to find us? I know she won't win as bad always loses against good. Evil can only enter a person when they are invited to enter. We must spread the news to everyone, to fight with the only weapon they have and need, a no entry sign in their souls to all evil. She will lose and be even more deranged."

I felt relieved as I knew even Incubus said the same thing. Demons can only enter through invitations from a soul. We could spread the message and save all the men and women who were being chased down by Alice the Succubus. Her only power came from us, the humans, accepting demons as danger and allowing our fears to rule through which they rule. I hugged my mother as we all knew all we had to do was not let our fears take over us.

We all said, "Where there is fear, there is horror. Yet faith gives birth to the end of all evil."

It was as if earlier, we had been imprisoned by the fear of what the demoness would do or when she would attack us. We knew there was nothing else to fear anymore. Death ends everything and life is blessed with hope and faith. So, everything else we would solve. We needed to find the mirror where her main soul was in and break it. Until then, we had to make sure not another innocent soul would be tormented by Alice the Succubus, nor would she be able to enter another innocent soul.

Tara Bella, my sister-in-law who was imprisoned by Succubus, stood up and hugged Aunt Marinda as she said, "I was scared. I kept seeing the demoness in my dreams. She told me I would never have a child of my own. She cursed me and said she would come back for me as I was her prisoner, and she wants to freeze me back in time. I don't care about myself anymore as I have Andries, my husband, and all of you my family members. I wanted to see you and Uncle Kees unite. Now I have lived my complete life."

Tara Bella walked up to a mirror and touched the mirror. She knew in her heart that we understood what she was going through. Alice was spying on us through the mirrors. Somehow, she could get into all and any home through mirrors. For me, it was a eureka moment as we realized how she always knew where we were, and what we were talking about.

Katelijne held on to Tara Bella as Tara Bella walked to the mirror and said, "I promise until my last breath, I will fight you for keeping Aunt Marinda and Uncle Kees apart. You broke a house, you broke a marriage, and you broke the temple of pure love by separating twin flames. I curse you to be without any twin flame, any love, or any peace. May you suffer hundred scores more for each person you have tormented. May my curses befall you as I too am one of your victims."

Katelijne cried as she hugged Tara Bella, and I saw Margriete run and hold on to Tara Bella and Katelijne. The three sisters-in-law hugged each other. Mama smiled as she teared up at the same time.

Mama said, "My three daughters are my pride and joy, not daughters-in-law but only daughters in this household. We are all brave and we fear nothing. Our boldness will be the saving grace of all the women who were victims of the demoness."

Again, like a thunderbolt we heard a woman shriek as she said, "No one gets rid of me. I will torment you all to your last breath."

My courageous Aunt Marinda said, "Let the war begin Alice the Succubus for even your demon husband, Daemon the Incubus, has left you. You should be ashamed of yourself. You have tried to separate twin flames by intoxication which you failed as the only twin flames you separated was yourself from your evil demon husband."

Alice screamed as we heard a male voice laugh and was overjoyed at his own laughter.

Daemon said with joy and pride in his voice, "I am a demon, true, but I too have my standards. Never could I think a mother would torment her own son and his lineage for anything unless you are an animal who eats her own children."

Daemon the Incubus laughed, and his laugh was scary as it woke up everyone in the hotel around us and in the whole neighborhood. I was scared if people would link us to these weird demons and ruin our family reputation. It was then I felt Mama's hand come hit my head. I wondered how she always read my mind. She just gave me a look and my two brothers were laughing with joy as they saw I was in trouble for thinking in my mind.

Daemon continued, "You're not welcome in the demonic world anymore, sweetheart. The news is you have been exiled from even this world. I hope you can find a real home and not have to live in other people's mirrors, for then remember your ugly face would be portrayed in everyone's homes. That is not something I would frame and not something you would want to see. For when a child or another woman sees your face in the mirror, they won't be scared as they would know anyone else is prettier than you. So, you would actually make their day."

Daemon then was silent as we heard screeches from an ugly demoness break out in the open daylight hours of a beautiful fog-free London morning. These days, the residents of greater London were all living in fear. Everyone knew a demonic person was on the loose who tormented and killed girls and boys alike. The demoness froze the bodies as life was sucked away from each of her victims. The sight was horrifying as no one knew who or what we were all fighting.

Daemon then said, "You all are correct as no demon can enter without permission. So, don't invite evil. It's that easy. Make sure that all the entry ports Succubus uses are closed. I will guide you to the other mirrors she uses. Even though the last one is going to be hard, one person will be able to break it in due time. Until then, spread the word. Don't invite evil into your home. Clear your mind, body, and soul."

That night, we sent Aunt Marinda and Uncle Kees home to Kasteel Vrederic in Naarden. We had a quick stopover in New York. On our journey, we received two blissful gifts to take home with us, yet with a lot of pain and sorrow. Then, we went back to Egypt in quest of finding the famous doctors, Dr. Smith and Dr. Avyaan, who we thought were in London but were nowhere to be found. When we returned to Egypt, we were told no one had ever heard of these two doctors.

Mama held on to the two precious gifts as she said to all of us, "Please be careful. I don't want any one of you carrying any mirrors with us on our trip back home to Naarden. I can't wait to be back home. I want to sleep in my own bed without any screeching or screams for a while."

Little did we know even at home waiting for us were enemies who were even banned from the demonic world. Visible enemies and visible wars we could fight, yet I wondered how we would fight the invisible war.

THE INVISIBLE WAR

Tormented and tortured,

Yet the signs of

Violence and ferocity

Were nowhere

To be seen or found

By any onlookers.

This war was

In between

The world known and

The world believed

To not even exist.

This world does exist

As the tormentors

Of this world

Are called demons.

They are known as vampires.

They are at times

Called witches.

The truth remains.

This unknown world,

Where the demonic

Tormentors hide

Are all in our world,

And the world

Not known to us,

Yet is so well known

And traveled

By these evil tyrants.

If we, the humans,

Could only see

These instigators

Only know to instigate.

We the innocent,

The most powerful,

Know how to

Eliminate the problem.

So,

We the agonized

Win against the agonies

Through

THE INVISIBLE WAR.

CHAPTER EIGHT:

DEMONIC WORLD'S CURSE

"A mother's defense and
A wife's pledge
Protect all as the
Prevalent
Blessings are
A woman's
Sanctifications,
Yet the vilest curses
Are also those
Of a female who is cursed
For her own evilness."

T he journey back home was filled with joy and happiness. It was also filled with a lot of tears and sadness. We returned home with Tara Bella's children, surprise gifts given to a mother from a mother who herself was only a child.

This surprise gift filled with painful tears are written within a new diary within the world of Kasteel Vrederic, which you can read within *Shattered Wings: Diary Of A Child Bride*.

The flight back home was frightening as we found ourselves in a dangerous situation. We suddenly had so much turbulence which caused a bumpy ride and made our plane rapidly begin to drop and lose altitude. Papa was not the pilot as his plane had taken Aunt Marinda and Uncle Kees home to Naarden. We used a direct commercial flight. All the passengers on board started to shout and scream in fear.

Mama got up and said to all the passengers, "Just be quiet everyone. If we are all dying from a plane crash, then let's enjoy the ride as we are all together. If any of you, however, want to survive, then remain calm and follow the instructions given by the flight attendants."

No flight attendants came. No one announced anything over the speakers. Papa got up and went to the front cabin where he saw the entire flight crew sleeping. The pilot and copilot were both sleeping. There were mirrors in the hands of the flight attendants as they had been getting ready for landing. Papa and Andries took over the pilot and copilot chairs. Andries reassured everyone we were all safe and would be starting to land soon. He asked the crew members to prepare for landing.

No flight attendants were awake, so Margriete and I assisted them to wake up. My sisters-in-law and some passengers also helped. We landed safely and the report was confusing. The report said some kind of interior gas leak caused all the crew members to fall asleep. Strangely, all the passengers were awake.

We knew the true story as we heard a laughter break out as the demoness said, "Next time you won't be so lucky. Your daughters are also under my radar Tara Bella, as you belong to me. You are my prisoner, and I might take both your daughters since you escaped."

Tara Bella was rescued from Malibu as Andries wrote in his diary, *The Immortality Serum: Vows From The Beyond*. I saw a different Tara Bella today as she stood up and tried to see where the words were coming from. She did not screech or cry in fear.

Tara Bella only said, "You are a mother who gave up your child. Today, I have my two adopted daughters as their birth mother who protected them with her last breath lost the battle of life to death. She won as a mother for she knew her girls today have a mother who will protect them eternally. My daughters have the blessings and protection of two mothers, their birth and adoptive. You can never touch them for a mother's love will burn you as you had given up motherhood for lust and greed."

Theunis got up and went to Tara Bella. He kissed the two babies we had brought back with us from our adventure in New York.

He then said to the girls, "You two will forever be under the protection of this friend."

Succubus the demoness had just begun her war with a mother, not a prisoner whom she had unjustly kept imprisoned. Mama and Papa hugged Tara Bella who was holding both her daughters, her newborn and her toddler. She kissed them and placed them in their car seats on the chairs next to her. They both went to sleep.

Our plane landed safely at Amsterdam Airport Schiphol. Papa handled all the logistics and news reporters who crowded the airport. We all left the airport without being noticed by any reporters. What waited for us in our home was also a big surprise, as we didn't let anyone in our home know about our two bundles of joy.

I enjoy traveling around the world, but I get homesick every time I travel. As we entered our home, Kasteel Vrederic, we realized how homesick we had all become. Andries, the new father, hugged the walls of our home. Antonius and I followed him as did Papa.

Somehow, I felt a cold shiver slide down my spine, and I felt we were in the sixteenth century. In front of our home was a coffin and a man was crying over the dead body. In the daylight hours, I thought I saw a woman dressed in all black scream and shout.

She was floating in the air as she screamed, "I will make sure every single person in this house is wiped out of existence even if it is the only and last thing I do."

Everyone froze and knew we were all being shown a mirage. We saw a mirror appear and from within, Papa from the sixteenth century walked out. He stood there as he saw himself and saw Mama. He stood in front of Mama and just tried to see her for a while.

He uttered words very slowly, "If only I could have kept you in my time too. I am blessed to know I have finally found you, my beloved. I hope my love for you and my curses upon the demoness protect my family throughout time."

We all saw Papa from the sixteenth century like a lightning bolt enter the body of Papa in the present and faint. I caught him in my arms and knew it's not safe to let someone see oneself in the past or the future, for it could cause memory problems. So, we discovered why Papa had memory problems as he had traveled time to see Mama.

We all waited for Papa to recover as he slept in his own bed for the first time in a while. Mama was worried as she sat next to Papa watching him like she would think it's a sin to even blink. She didn't want to miss the moment he awakens.

Uncle Kees either thought or spoke out loud, "I am the reason Erasmus is having all this trouble. If only I had not come to Kasteel Vrederic or Marinda had not come, then maybe Erasmus would have been completely all right in his last life and this life."

Aunt Marinda and Uncle Kees walked around with guilt-filled agonies. Papa moved around and tried to shake himself up from his sleeping position. Mama held him in her arms as she supported his weight with her tiny petite body. Antonius, Andries, and I ran to help Mama.

Papa laughed out loud with so much elegance and dignity, we knew our father was back. He looked at all of us with so much love. As we all sat on Mama and Papa's bed, it felt like we were revisiting our childhood when all the problems in the world would just fade away if only our father was there.

He smiled as he laughingly said, "I am okay. It's strange because I had known this fact for ages but never realized. My last life's soul always visited this life's soul. I didn't lose my mind because for me it was normal. I had visited your mother in her dreams as she had visited me in my dreams the same way. Our souls are the same. Our Earthly vehicles are different. I'm assuming some people can travel time like we did in our dreams and at times in daylight hours."

I admired my parents so much. I knew we were all blessed to have both of them in this life. They both coauthored their love story together in the famous diary, *Be My Destiny: Vows From The Beyond*. I couldn't figure out the dreams and the time-traveling parts, but I knew it happened.

So, I assumed Papa had traveled time and knew he could find his beloved in the future. When he would go back in time and see she was missing, it's then he would lose his mind. He assumed he was crazy and was only dreaming or imagining about her and his family members.

I knew Aunt Marinda read my mind as she said, "No, Jacobus, we did not read your mind, but you spoke out loud."

I realized I always think out loud, like my brothers.

Papa sat up and said, "I always knew I had traveled time in my dreams and saw the future. I, the present man, had known all of this as I had traveled time to the past and seen my past form as you all did."

Aunt Marinda was walking out of the room as she stopped and said, "Tara Bella must be ready for her revenge. Succubus will try to harm her girls to get back at her. I'm so excited our Tara Bella has her girls. We must protect those two girls at any cost. They were blessings from one mother to another mother."

Margriete held on to the newborn baby Ahana Bella as Katelijne held on to the toddler Hana Bella in her arms.

Our new mother Tara Bella came and held my hands as she cried and whimpered, "Have I not suffered enough? Why does she want to harm my baby girls? They did nothing wrong to her. I don't know why she did this to me either. But I will place her in the glass coffin she had me in. For I know the only truth no one knows is that Succubus is scared of everything she puts her victims into, the glass coffin, the gallows, and the cremation grounds."

There in our home we heard cracks all around, as if something was being broken in anger.

Aunt Marinda jumped up as she said, "The demoness can't enter this house Erasmus. She is breaking all the mirrors so that I can't time travel. Or, when nightfall approaches, I will die as I have no mirror to be within. If all the mirrors are broken, then she the demoness would be free."

Our newborn baby girl Ahana Bella started to cry as did our toddler Hana Bella. The sounds were hurting their ears, and they were hurting our ears too. Margriete and I immediately placed noise-cancelling headphones on the babies. I knew they wouldn't protect the ears from all the noises, but they would alleviate the sounds somewhat, which would help the babies. Margriete also gave the baby a pacifier and gave the toddler a drink.

The children got busy trying to figure out the new headphones. The baby kept trying to move her head and the toddler tried to figure out what she had on her ears. They both forgot about the mirror cracking sounds.

Tara Bella got up and called Incubus as she said, "Please help a mother."

At that stage my mother and Aunt Marinda both placed their hands on Tara Bella's mouth.

Mama shook her head and said, "No, I won't have any demon or demoness enter my home for any reason at all. Don't ever extend any invitation to any demon even if you fear death to be near. Believe in me, death is not as scary as being hunted or being indebted to a demon."

Tara Bella hugged Mama and cried as she calmed herself down. We all sat down as I saw in front of us were standing our four children, Theunis, Alexander, Griet, and Rietje, the founding members of Kasteel Vrederic.

Theunis laughed as he said in his very childish voice, "Don't fear, I'm here. Let her break all the mirrors of this world. She fears being imprisoned in a mirror as the prophecy was, she would be imprisoned for life in one. So, she imprisons all who she bullies in mirrors, and she keeps a mirror to travel through and not be imprisoned within."

Theunis smiled and hugged the new babies as he kissed their heads and blessed them with his hands.

He then said, "Aunt Marinda would die if all the mirrors were broken before Aunt Marinda's complete soul can be freed from Succubus's curses. Aunt Marinda being a time traveler needs the mirrors to travel time and help all whom Succubus victimizes. They both need mirrors, but

Succubus doesn't want anyone else to have the powers of a mirror."

I didn't know what was happening but knew somehow, we had to save a mirror from breaking for Aunt Marinda. How would we save one for her? We witnessed a miracle was happening as Tara Bella cried and poured innocent tears for her babies and Aunt Marinda.

She blamed herself and kept repeating, "My freedom released this demoness. It's all my fault."

Theunis was still watching her as I realized the child Theunis had a hard time comprehending all the adult words. For some reason, he didn't change his form always but only at certain times.

Theunis placed his hands under Tara Bella's eyes as he caught her tears. Then, he blew something on his hands. I saw the tears had become mirrors as Theunis laughed and gave two newly created mirrors to Tara Bella.

He said, "One is for you to imprison Alice the Succubus so she never escapes. The other one is for Aunt Marinda to be safe and the only face for all children or people to see when they need help or protection from the most beautiful, pure, and kind woman, our Aunt Marinda, the woman who chose to be imprisoned in the mirror to be of help to all the others who need help even though she had to be separated from her beloved to do so."

As long as we had the father of the lighthouse of Kasteel Vrederic with us, no one could harm our family home. Theunis himself had gifted the lighthouse of Kasteel Vrederic centuries ago and could create mirrors from the blessed tears of all innocent eyes.

We saw all of the other mirrors in our home break as a news alert reported mirrors around the world were breaking because of a strange phenomenon. The tear-created mirrors remained intact. The news repeated scientists around the world were linking this to some kind of weather change and some kind of magnetic source.

It was strange to see the whole world face the same crisis and I felt guilty if this was because of us. I could forgive everything else but not being the reason of someone else's troubles or harm.

I said to Theunis and Griet, "Dear children, it hurts me beyond anything if even a single person is hurt because of our family's personal enemies."

Griet jumped up and came running to me. She put her little hands gesturing to me like she does when she wants me to carry her. I placed her in my arms as I kissed her cheeks, and she kissed mine.

She said, "Silly Papa Jacobus. Don't worry and never fear for at all times, see the lighthouse is there still guiding us."

Griet pointed her small, soft, and chubby finger toward the lighthouse.

Uncle Kees suddenly stood up and screamed as he asked, "What's going on? Why is there a couple kissing in the lighthouse? Did someone break into our home Erasmus?"

Aunt Marinda was trying to see what Uncle Kees was talking about as she froze and just bewilderedly stared at her husband. I knew true love when I saw and felt it.

Papa told Uncle Kees, "Today after years, twin flames have found one another and for that reason, the lovebirds, Griet and Theunis's sixteenth-century forms, reappeared in the lighthouse. The famous legend of the lighthouse is that only true twin flames are able to see them when they stand in front of the lighthouse together."

I felt relieved and was overjoyed with happiness. The aunt I loved and admired for centuries finally found her twin flame, her beloved. Mama was teared up as was Papa at this once-in-a-lifetime sight we would treasure and remember forever.

The sun set at our home Kasteel Vrederic as we heard the gushing waters in the river behind our home. The miraculous sounds of the water running and the birds singing around our home were amazing. The courtyard in front of our home was glowing from the lighthouse that had been sitting on top of our home for centuries. This lighthouse always had the sixteenth century's kissing couple Theunis and Griet in it, protecting our home throughout time.

My whole family even Papa who now looked and felt completely healed was glued to the television screen. We got a phone call which broke the silence as we all jerked up. It was strange as we have faced so many horrific paranormal activities, we would think it was normal by now. It never got normal, but by now it was a part of our life.

Papa answered the phone as my brothers hovered over him, trying to listen in. Mama gestured Papa to place his phone on speakerphone. He did and we heard a man who at times existed and at times no one knew who he was. Dr. Avyaan's voice could be heard clearly on speakerphone.

Dr. Avyaan said, "I was hoping to catch Dr. Jacobus today. I really need to talk to him. It's extremely urgent that I do so."

Papa gestured toward me as he asked with his body language if I would answer the phone, or if I wanted him to talk. I signaled back for him to continue, and I would only speak if I thought I had to.

Papa said, "The famous Dr. Avyaan, what a pleasure it is to hear from you. I know my son was looking for you, but I hear you are the desert's mirage. You only appear when it's extremely hot and deadly, yet you are just a figment of the mind's imagination. So, I will hang up as I must be imagining your calls and actually in reality you never called."

I heard a chuckle on the other side. It was one of those weird, spooky, annoying, nail-scratching chuckles. Even though you want to shout and tell them to be normal, you don't want to offend them by saying it. The worst part was this person was always a good friend and helping hand to Margriete and myself, whenever we needed him.

He said, "I know Jacobus is there and you are all listening in through the speakerphone. I will only say that you all call me Daemon, but my other name is Dr. Avyaan. This is my human form in this life, just like Alice is Succubus's human form. In this life, I have tried to change my image and my personality as I don't like being bad or doing evil. I have tried to help the humans and the animal world as much as possible."

I stood up as did all my family members.

Margriete was shocked as she started to scream, "What in the world are you saying? You sent us on a goose chase everywhere knowing what we would face and the risks we would take."

Mama told Margriete not to show her temper or feelings to a demon, even if he was trying to change his own path.

Dr. Avyaan said, "Humans change and get a second chance in life, so I too wanted to give my immortal life a second chance. Why can't I be good or try to be good if I can get a second chance? Is it not true Anadhi that good wins the battle over evil?"

Mama was shocked how he called her directly by name. She glared at Papa as he told her not to engage in a war of words with a demon. Yet we all knew Mama would be Mama.

She said, "Yes, I believe good will always be victorious. That's why I know you will lose, because you can't try to be good but just be good. When you realize you want to be good, yet you still struggle, it means you are willingly doing evil. By pretending or just trying to change your image if you even happen to do some good, that's good for you. Remember never ever use my family to do so or for your evil wife's doings."

Papa laughed quietly as he kissed Mama and hugged her. I was shaking in fear of what my mother would say and felt relieved after the discussion.

Dr. Avyaan said, "I don't know when I started becoming more like Incubus and less of a doctor. I must say I have never placed any one of my patients' life or my research at risk, but I have actually solved so many miraculous cases only because of who I am."

I felt a fire boil through my whole body when I heard him talk. He placed my family at risk by sending us to different places and even by rescuing our family when we needed to be rescued. I must never forget it was he who had placed us in danger. Our freedom of doing things our own way was under attack. Yet I thought to myself, I would use him to do some good, before we place him and his evil wife inside of a mirror again where they can never do any harm.

As we were all talking, Theunis asked Dr. Avyaan, "Where did you appear from? How did you become Dr. Avyaan if you were never born or brought out by a time traveler? As a direct descendant, I ask you the question. You must oblige by answering."

Like thunder, we heard a loud bang on top of our home. Then, we saw on the television screen, a movie we never ordered was playing.

A well-stocked farmer's market was taking place somewhere in London. We saw on the screen, people were rushing to get good deals on homemade cheese, jam, bread, and butter. There was an antique store where people were trying to get bargains.

The sign on top of a place read Camden Market. There were diverse community members walking hand in hand. It was a bright Saturday morning. Children and adults were enjoying the street food, trading, and just strolling by the Regent's Canal nearby. This market was happening in a historical Central London location.

I worried for the crowd as I knew somehow a form of the demon, Incubus, was there. After surveying the area carefully, I saw someone who was bargaining for a portrait of a war veteran. The very strange portrait was sketched on a mirror. It glowed in the open daylight hours. The fear of buying an old antique painting never touched the buyers or the sellers.

There was a young man who wanted to buy the painting as he said to the others who wanted the same painting, "I am a medical student who needs a break every now and then. If you guys don't really need the painting, then I will buy it."

The crowd cheered for him, as someone from the crowd said, "Thank you for being there. We will always remember how you had been there for us. Now we shall be there for you."

In the mirror was Incubus. He winked at us even from the painting. He was just sitting on a chair which looked like a throne. I saw the chair throw Incubus into the air.

It was then we saw a very angry demon who looked like a man say, "Who dare does this to me? Why have I been kicked off my throne?"

I tried to inspect the picture very closely. The man walked out of the painting and entered the young doctor's physical body. I felt like we were on a movie set. I saw in an open farmer's market, Incubus traveled time and entered the body of a young doctor named Dr. Hans Avyaan.

The famous doctor could neither talk, nor did he say anything. We all realized Incubus had just entered a human's body. Through this human body, he would live, yet he would rule on Earth through his evil demon body.

Behind the portrait, we saw a picture of a child. The child had a piece of a mirror in one hand, and with the other hand, he was erasing the picture within the mirror. The woman in the painting was trying to slice the child with a piece of the broken mirror. She sliced the painting but could do nothing to the child. The mirror just broke into pieces. The man and the woman exited the painting and just disappeared. The child, however, was just there. I knew no one saw this except for my family. From the television screen, we witnessed history.

Incubus the demon told Succubus the demoness, "I challenge you to ruin yourself and be buried within this same mirror you had imprisoned so many within. You are proof a woman cannot be a mother just by giving birth but by raising a child. All shall know how you are an embarrassment for all universes combined. You will be imprisoned within this mirror. I will leave you behind for my son to recover and find. You tried to kill your own son with the broken mirror piece, but you stupid demoness should know you can't kill an immortal. You should know that for him, you will be mortal."

Incubus the demon was angry as he threw his fist on the wall next to where he was standing. He shook the demoness as he saw her with so much disgust. It gave me the shivers.

He then said "I know even animals takes care of their own, but you do not. You are so ugly because motherhood, be it an adoptive mother or a biological mother, makes a woman beautiful, demon or human. So, I curse you eternally to be hunted down by your own greed. Don't forget, I too am as evil as you are if not more. Yet for going after my biological son, your own blood, I curse you to be eternally buried within a mirror and be known to all as the ugliest woman in the universe who could not even love her own son."

Incubus made direct eye contact with us, bent his head, and gave a thumbs up sign acknowledging he knew the future and that we would see the video.

He said looking at the screen, "I, the demon known to be Dr. Avyaan, Daemon, or to some as Incubus, hereby curse my wife, the demoness, known as Alice or Succubus, to be unhappy and hunted down by the blood of the living or dead human family our son chose to be within and protect with his own life. May they be able to imprison you the immortal demoness even though the humans are but mortals. Let the war be of evil against good. Let this war be known as the demonic world's curse. Don't forget to find the mirror with the sketch. It will never break and it's your only protection. Let this war be known as the demonic world's curse."

DEMONIC WORLD'S CURSE

Vengeance is

Filled with

Anger and unjust.

Revenge is a fruition

Of unjust and anger.

Yet what is forgiveness?

Within humans, forgiveness is given.

Within humanity,

Forgiveness prevails.

Yet within

The land of demons,

Within the land of terror,

Forgiveness is missing.

So, if you are fighting

A demon within human physique,

Within human frame,

Know what you will face.

Know what you will be confronting

If you befriend,

Or assist a demon,

Be it is

In spiritual

Or human form.

Let go of

The demonic behaviors and manners,

And become

The most powerful

Source and weapon

Who can take upon

And fight the demons,

And the demonic actions

Of a man or demon alike.

Never, ever fall prey,

To the false promises

Of a demon.

As always,

Remember

When you the human

Take upon

The demonic worlds,

At all times,

At all places,

You will face bitterness,

And you will face anger.

Unless you

Have the

Love and blessings

Of a mother,

For even a demon

Respects a mother's love,

For they know

If they go against

A mother's love,

They will burn themselves

To ashes.

If a mother becomes

A demon or

A predator,

Then even the

World above

And beyond

Will never forgive

The mother

Who is the snake woman,

Who shall eternally

Be cursed

By Heavens above

To always have

A cursed life

Within Earth

Or the beyond.

Even the worst

Of the worst

Will not forgive

A mother who betrays

Her own children.

You the cursed mother will face

Vengeance and retribution,

From good and from evil

As all good and bad

Have animosity against you.

You shall be under

The Heaven's

The universe's,

And the

DEMONIC WORLD'S CURSE.

CHAPTER NINE:

THEUNIS, THE FATHER OF THE LIGHTHOUSE

"Love lives on beyond
Life or even death.
Vows made and kept,
In life, in death, or
In rebirth,
Confirm a beloved
As the father
Of the family tree."

Flames of fear spread nothing but unrest. We were told a lot of unrest and fear had gripped all over the world as London, New York, and Egypt had unnatural abductions and deaths of women and men. The authorities tried to make these unnatural happenings seem like a man, woman, or a huge group was at the core of it. They reassured all they wouldn't rest until all these abductions and unsolved cases were solved.

Theunis's story was bothering me as I knew he was somehow born in this world. Yet how did he appear in the portrait? I witnessed a child being tormented by his demonic mother through a mirror in a portrait. Even though she never knew his physical body, it amazed me she was still his mother. I guess it's not the biological mother who develops a child's character but the mother who brings the child up.

Margriete walked in with Theunis as she said, "I tried to put the boys to bed. Every time I try, my little boys refuse to sleep. Theunis has been crying nonstop. I asked Alexander what was wrong with him, but Alexander joined him in the crying. Someone, please help my boys. What's going on?"

I ran up to our brave Theunis and lifted him up in my arms. I remembered how we were buddies in one lifetime when he had married my daughter. Today, I held him in my arms as I saw my daughter Rietje and my niece Griet walk into the family room. Katelijne walked in with the girls as she was trying to put them to bed.

Papa and Mama took the girls as they placed them on their laps and kissed the girls. Margriete was trying to calm the boys down as Antonius and Andries took over. Andries felt awful seeing the boys spill tears and kissed both as Antonius wiped off their falling tears.

Alexander said in his childish voice, "We are scared. What if Succubus harms our family? What about Aunt Marinda and Uncle Kees? What about the new baby girls, Ahana Bella and Hana Bella? They didn't do anything wrong. They are just babies. We are just children. Why does she want to kill my buddy Theunis and us?"

Our two girls Griet and Rietje joined the boys and started to cry. Our four brave young children had taken upon themselves burdens, mysteries, time traveling, and paranormal activities like soldiers. When I see them at night or when they are all ready to sleep, they become just kids. It's shocking even though these four are children, they have taken on far more responsibilities than what adults could ever take in forget one, but numerous lifetimes.

For this reason, I am glad my whole family makes sure these miraculous children get a childhood as normal as possible. Maybe in this family, this is normal. Beyond everything, we love one another more than one lifetime as we have crossed over to be with one another and it shows.

Tara Bella was holding on to her toddler in her arms as she had the baby in a kangaroo pouch. I knew yawning was contagious but today I saw crying was too. Both Hana Bella and Ahana Bella joined the group of crying babies.

Andries then said, "In this household, I am the only young one. All of you babies come after me. Mama, tell them no one cries in this household because we choose laughing over crying."

Mama scowled at Andries, and I knew he had it coming. She gave him the look. My brothers and I knew never to get that look, for even now I freeze thinking I must have done something for Mama to be upset. Automatically, we kissed Mama.

She said, "My brave babies, all of you remember in this household we shall only be happy, not sad. Celebrate life, and death is not scary. When we can't solve a problem we face, we take a break and get back to it another dawn. Everything looks scary at night, but somehow the troubles resolve on their own after dawn."

Mama worried her words were getting lost and not reaching the babies and the children as they were still frightened. She didn't think they comprehended the whole message. I knew, however, she knew these kids understood more than we the adults could even comprehend.

Mama said, "Aunt Marinda, please help."

Uncle Kees and Aunt Marinda were both watching the boys for a while. Aunt Marinda walked over to the boys. Her hair which was a mix of brown and blonde was blowing in the air. She looked different from her last form as traveling time changes a person's appearance.

She wore a white and blue dress which made her look like a fairy. I know how much I love Aunt Marinda, but every time I see her, I realize I love her more. She was my only support when there was no one. She loves and gives without ever saying anything.

She walked and came close to me as she kissed my head and said, "I love you more Jacobus, and always will. Also, boys, never fear we are all together here. We will all be just all right. I promise."

Theunis and Alexander ran and hugged the woman they had known as their adoptive mother figure all their lives. She laughed and grabbed both boys in her arms as she kissed them both on their opposite cheeks. She was laughing and they were both laughing with her. Griet and Rietje ran to Aunt Marinda and kissed her on her cheeks. This was a different kind of family reunion, bound through time and through the bond of eternal and evermore love.

Finally, it became true. A reunion that had been in the happening for centuries. Tears became laughter as all four children who had been with Aunt Marinda were rejoicing their long-awaited reunion. I realized it's not about being a biological father or mother as I was Griet's biological father in the sixteenth century yet now through the door of reincarnation, I became her uncle and Rietje's biological father. It was Aunt Marinda who has been raising all these children for centuries. We only have them today, because our Aunt Marinda had sacrificed her own love, her life, to always be there for all of us.

Theunis guarded all of us as he stood up and in front of me, I saw a grown-up man standing. Theunis made eye contact with the other three and signaled to them not to do anything but get behind Aunt Marinda.

Theunis said, "Aunt Marinda, the lighthouse has been giving signals to warn us evil is around. We must find the last mirror and break it, so that Alice's physical body will be free from being hunted by Succubus the demon. Alice is not evil unlike the real demonesses. She was taken over by Succubus, the woman who had given birth to me. She wants me to be mortal and dead, so that's what she is hunting innocent souls for."

Aunt Marinda sat down on the couch and closed her eyes. She said without opening her eyes, "Very noble of you, my dear child. The truth is she only wants you so she can be immortal. With your birth, both your biological parents will only be time travelers, not real physical demons. Your world had exiled both, because you have taken over and told all to be good with all humans. So, they are both living through other human bodies."

Mama sat on the couch. She looked tired but was only thinking about everyone else except herself. Papa sat by her as he hugged her. Uncle Kees stood in the corner just watching the stars above the night skies.

Uncle Kees said, "I thought I had fallen in love with a fair maiden and would live a simple life. It turned out my wife who was a celibate virgin was related to a sex demoness who only wanted to ruin all on her path."

Papa got up and ran toward the children. He tried to cover the ears of all the children. He gave Uncle Kees a very scary face as he said, "Kees, we have children in the home. Please only words we are allowed to say in front of them."

Andries laughed and was having a fit watching Uncle Kees being scolded at. Uncle Kees hugged the children and gave all of them kisses on their cheeks.

Theunis was still standing in the middle of the room listening to all of this as he said, "Please everyone, we must find out where the last mirror is hidden. It's urgent! Otherwise, Alice will be dead soon, and the demoness will find another body to enter and do her deeds. We wouldn't know then which body she is hiding within. Also, don't trust Dr. Avyaan or Daemon the Incubus, for he too will hunt for a body unless he is forgiven and allowed to reenter the demon world. I probably will forgive him and give him a second chance so he can help us."

It was then, our whole house quivered like we were having an earthquake. There were glass breaking sounds as all the windows around the house were shattering. The horses in our barn were whining.

All I could think about was I had to protect Aunt Marinda and Uncle Kees. Papa beat me and my brothers as he jumped up, hugged Uncle Kees, and screamed, "Hold Aunt Marinda everyone! Make sure my brother and his wife are safe! Please Theunis, do something!"

I held Aunt Marinda in my chest as my two brothers ran around the house trying to see what was going on. A doorbell awakened all of us from our frozen state.

Bertelmeeus entered our home in a frantic panic asking, "All right everyone, what are you all up to? The whole Naarden felt the earthquake. I know it must be something paranormal as my Kasteel Vrederic family members are involved."

He ran to Aunt Marinda in exhilaration as he finally saw his sister from centuries ago.

He said, "Biological or not, you are my sister. Are you here or traveling time again? If I could get my previous life's memories to guide me, I remember that man. He was your husband who had come for your coffin. Your time-traveling body told me to never tell this story to anyone. I died with this truth in my soul and am blessed I have my memories to guide you in this life."

Everything went silent and we knew somehow, Succubus was listening in. She wanted the mirror Bertelmeeus had hidden in the sixteenth century. We all thought he had hidden it with the diary in Aunt Marinda's coffin, but did he remove it and place it somewhere else?

Bertelmeeus held Theunis and Alexander. He hugged them both as he picked up Griet in his arms and kissed her. He then picked up Rietje and hugged her. He touched her face and kissed her cheeks.

He said, "Little one, this great-uncle of yours still breathes for you. You were and still are my heartbeats. Yes, little one my heart beats your name even in this century. With Jacobus, I raised you and even in this life I still feel like it was just yesterday."

He surveyed her for a while and made a head gesture as I knew these two had a secret they shared. My young child saw Theunis and just kept on smiling.

She kissed Bertelmeeus back on both of his cheeks and said, "My heart beats Great-Uncle Bertelmeeus's name too."

I felt like a piece of my soul was crying as I knew in the century when I was Jacobus van Vrederic, the diarist, this was a phrase Rietje and I used for one another. Yet then I was her Opa and now her father. Time and reincarnation change so many relationships yet never does it take away eternal love and love stories. For time wipes away everything yet true love stories written through lovers, a father and a daughter, or even a grandfather and his granddaughter, never fade nor do they die.

Griet and Rietje both came and hugged me as if they knew I was recalling our previous life stories, some of which was written, but a lot faded away through the reincarnated oceans of life. I felt the heartbeats of two girls and knew we were all going to have to face yet another war.

I asked Rietje, "Baby girl, do you know what we are all looking for? Did Bertelmeeus give you anything to hide. Or did Griet or Theunis give you something to hide?"

I saw she was observing Theunis as she asked him for his permission. I realized she too knew who he was from her last life. She then saw Margriete and asked her something with her eyes. The whole thing was so strange as if I was in the room but somehow was missing from all of these secrets.

Theunis said, "I had given something to Rietje to hide in the sixteenth century. The last mirror was given to me by Aunt Marinda's traveling form. I kept it with me for a long time, but as everyone left through the reincarnation tunnel, I gave it to Rietje."

We all simultaneously looked at Rietje. We knew the last mirror where Aunt Marinda's soul was, and the only mirror Alice the Succubus wanted, was hidden in our home. The mirror Aunt Marinda had kept with her in the coffin was hidden somewhere by Rietje. I assumed Aunt Marinda had given the mirror to Theunis to hide and keep safe, so our family could free Aunt Marinda and finally get rid of Alice the Succubus.

The lighthouse that had been on top of our home from the sixteenth century since Theunis had installed it, had turned on. The front and back courtyards were brightened with ever glowing magical embers. This lighthouse had guided our family members for centuries. I knew everyone in our household knew where Rietje had hidden the mirror.

She just saw Theunis and laughed as she said to me, "Silly Papa, the lighthouse is made out of it. Remember, Griet and Theunis made the lighthouse with it. The evil lady can never enter the mirror through here because she will burn to ashes, but Aunt Marinda can always come through it."

Theunis laughed and went and hugged Rietje the child as he was in an adult form. All the family members on this day were descendants of Rietje and Alexander, as Rietje was the only living child of my daughter, Griet and her husband Theunis. So, the whole family tree continued and grew from Theunis. Our family was being protected all these years through the lighthouse he had made and placed on top of Kasteel Vrederic.

Suddenly, Theunis laughed and said, "The evil woman tried to follow us in search of the last mirror she could use to stay in this century or travel to other time zones.

All her other transporting mirrors were broken. This lighthouse has taken her back to centuries ago when she had tried and killed Aunt Marinda and Uncle Kees. Now, she will be stuck there forever unless we too travel time and prevent her from ever traveling time to kill."

I got up and smiled as we all felt a sudden peace in our minds realizing the woman was really stuck in the sixteenth century. We know she wanted to go there because she wanted to change our future. Yet Theunis had known this and preplanned this as he is and shall always be known as Theunis, the father of the lighthouse.

THEUNIS, THE FATHER OF THE LIGHTHOUSE

Born from the world of demons,

You arrived on Earth

Through human bodies,

Thought to be

Dreadfully evil,

Filled with only avenge.

Yet you became,

The honorable,

The devout, and

The sincere husband.

As you found true love,

You found your true self,

Not just within

Your own body,

But through

The union of

True twin flames.

You burned your soul

To be only

The righteous husband,

The virtuous father

Of the only

Surviving descendant

Of Kasteel Vrederic.

You are not just your daughter's

But all your descendants'

Forefather

As we all call

And respect you,

As

THEUNIS, THE FATHER OF THE LIGHTHOUSE.

CHAPTER TEN:

WOMAN IN THE MIRROR

"Fear the face
You don't see,
Yet accept the face
You do see
In the mirror
Only when
You are standing
In front of the mirror."

Fear imprisons a person. It grips a person into a space where you the person feel like you have been shackled and you can't move. It is somewhat similar to sleep paralysis. I, you could say, am lucky. My ancestors roam around this house and protect all their descendants within the walls of Kasteel Vrederic.

The rule is never fear for we are here. You might ask, but are they not ghosts? My answer is yes and no. You see, some are our own previous incarnations from our past lives. They are there, yet they are not. As a time-traveling family, we can go back in time and see ourselves there without confronting ourselves. I will tell you in the world of reincarnation where faith walks with the travelers, no one is a ghost, only time travelers through the door of reincarnation.

We have all taken an oath where we say, we will not be scared, nor will we be imprisoned by fear. For what is there to fear when at the end you have another chance in life through the door of reincarnation?

Margriete and I went to bed after staying awake for most of the night. Dawn was peeking through the windows. It seemed like sunrise. Instead of the world getting evolved within darkness, the world was being greeted by the rays of the early morning light of dawn. Meanwhile, my wife just sat on the bed staring at the fireplace. The amber-colored fire from the fireplace was lovely. It was burning on the side to keep the room warm and not freezing. My wife loves to keep the windows ajar while the white curtains dance in the crisp winter air. Somehow, I too am so used to her ways. These simple actions of my wife make the room feel like Heaven. It felt good to be back home.

I forgot my beautiful wife was sitting next to me and wanted me to pay her some attention. I nodded in agreement as she was waiting for an answer. Yes, she could read my mind or just being with me knew my ways as I knew her ways. How could I tell her she was always in my mind, in my awakening state, and in my sleeping state?

I wanted to ask her what was bothering her. Yet where would I start? Our life together did not start with this life but at least two lifetimes that I could remember. Both times it was hard for Margriete, but she never complained and never said anything. My wife squinted her eyes and looked to her fingers as she does when she becomes shy.

She said, "Sweetheart, it's a wonderful life with you eternally. With all the paranormal activities we have been through together, it feels like there is nothing we can't do if we are together. I was just wondering about Aunt Marinda and Uncle Kees. I want to give them a small wedding where they can renew their vows. I keep remembering a mirror that I had seen or had, but I can't somehow get it. It's like when you have a thought, but just go blank."

Yes, I knew the going blank feeling. I laughed and hugged her in my arms. Always thinking about someone else, my wife is the most beautiful person in the world, inside and out. She looks more Indian than Dutch like my mother. Long black hair and olive-colored skin. Yet somehow, I would say she looks like Snow White, the fictional character whom Rietje and Griet love to read about.

That's when I followed her gaze and stared at a mirror hanging on top of our fireplace, the one Griet and Rietje gifted us on our last wedding anniversary. They both had said a friend helped them find it as it was in a box in our attic with other ancestral things. The mirror reminded them of Margriete and the image sketched on the mirror looked so much like her. The mirror pulled me toward it.

I pressed the intercom and screamed, "Mama, Papa, everyone come quickly please. You all said all the mirrors in the house broke in the unnatural paranormal earthquake. Then, why is the one hanging on our fireplace wall looking back at me like it's a portal and is alive?"

The wind picked up letting us know there was a storm brewing outside as well as a frightening storm brewing inside of our home. Margriete ran toward the nursery on the second floor where Rietje and Griet were sleeping. The cousins never left one another's side. Even in their sleep they would call out for one another.

I got up and closed the windows. For some reason, I didn't want anyone entering our home even though our bedroom was on the third floor, high above the ground level. These Gothic Dutch homes were constructed very well and the ceilings for each floor were fifteen feet tall.

I ran toward the boys' room as I met up with Mama and Papa gathering up the boys and saw my brothers were gathering everyone else. We all went to the girls' room where I saw Margriete, Katelijne, and Tara Bella gather up all four little girls.

Our newest additions were looking at us so innocently. The baby thought it was her feeding time and followed her mother Tara Bella with her big blue eyes and blonde hair. The toddler in Andries's arms went back to sleep so comfortably. They were by now used to waking up at weird hours and being rushed in and out of homes. I am assuming their little minds thought these paranormal activities were just normal.

Griet and Rietje were sleeping in Antonius's arms as Theunis and Alexander were both in Papa's arms. I wondered what was happening. Did I just panic for no reason? Guilt covered my whole body as I saw the sleeping children try to sleep after all the things we had gone through. I worried in my mind, why was my wife's picture sketched on the mirror? Why was the sketch more prominent now and we never realized before?

Aunt Marinda was drinking herbal tea as was Uncle Kees and Bertelmeeus. They all came back to Margriete's and my bedroom. We walked to the sitting room next to the bed chamber. The fireplace was still on, as Papa was trying to fix himself a drink from the small bar Margriete and I had in the library section of our room.

Papa who loved to drink looked upset as he found no alcoholic drinks in our bar. He gave me the look of annoyance and poured himself a glass of orange juice. I could only smile as he could have poured himself milk as this bar in our room only had kid-friendly juices or milk. After all, my wife is a pediatric cardiovascular surgeon and she always says, a mother first. Food, drinks, or anything and everything in this room must be kid friendly. No alcohol of any kind.

Papa gave me the look and said, "I am a grandfather and I deserve to have alcoholic drinks. Your mother and I enjoy some alcoholic drinks from time to time. Is this orange juice, normal juice, or baby juice of some kind?"

Margriete broke out into laughter as she eyed me and signaled me to tell him. Andries walked over and helped himself with some juice as he gave his toddler some to share.

Papa observed Andries, spat out the juice, and said, "Hmm baby juice bottles, I presume. I'm glad they were not breast milk. Your bars are filled with baby formula and breast milk. When has a bar turned into a baby fridge? It's safe to drink, correct?"

Mama gave Papa a blank stare as she shook her head and said, "Yes, safe for both adults and children. Ever since we had babies and now grandbabies Erasmus, we all store them in all of our rooms. Where were you all those years?

Mama turned to me and said, "Jacobus, give your father a beer please."

I gave Papa a can of beer. He took it from me and gave me the look. My very angry Papa went on our bed and adjusted himself on it. He got under the blanket, raised his eyebrows at us and asked, "Is this beer safe to drink?"

Everyone in the room helped themselves with small bottles of orange juice. Andries knew there were sugar-free, all natural low-carb bottles for diabetics in there as well.

Andries saw Papa and said, "Big Papa, I am having non-alcoholic orange juice made for children. Obviously, they are safe."

Papa grumbled and grunted and said something under his breath. Mama sighed and hollered at him.

Mama said, "Say it out loud. We're all worried about the grumbles coming out of the walls. Why are you adding sounds to them? It's impossible to differentiate yours from the ones in the walls."

I started to laugh at my parents. I knew they were having temper tantrums because we all were going through a lack of sleep.

It was then the whole house shook again and I could smell blood in my mouth. I kept thinking wrong time zone, must go even further. I felt like I was on the ground dying as I had been shot. Margriete was lying on top of me, crying she wouldn't let me go. Even in death, she would follow me. I was having some kind of shivers and shaking rigorously.

My mother was holding me as Margriete was taking my vitals. It was as if I had traveled to the past again and saw my own death all over again in the seventeenth century.

I shook myself up and told my mother, "Mama, why is it I keep on going back to the wrong time? I don't know why I was again seeing the horrific death of my past life yet somehow, I knew I was at the wrong time and must go back further to the time of Griet being born and to the time of her death. I must travel further back and not end up at the time of my death."

Papa came near me and held me with his hands. He gave his can of beer, and I had a sip. It gave me the boost I needed.

He told Andries, "You can have this one too, it's sugar-free."

In between everything, Margriete took the can and gave it to Antonius to drink as she said, "He can't have any more. He had one and he is a diabetic. So, here you go. You finish it. I don't want him having too many carbohydrates. Like I said, it's not just sugar, but you must calculate your carb intake."

Antonius finished the beer and said, "What's going on here? This is good beer. You really can't tell it's sugar free."

I told them about the mirror and showed everyone the mirror.

Margriete carried Griet toward the mirror and asked her, "Sweet child, what is this mirror? Rietje and you gave this to us. Where did you find this? Who helped you find it?"

Rietje jumped backward and looked at the mirror as she said, "I gave you this with cousin Griet. It's my gift to you, remember? When Opa Jacobus came to be with us last time, Papa Theunis gave me this to keep safe. So, you could take it back home, or else all of them would have been lost in the tunnel of light. You were my Oma and had died right after Opa. You died in front of this mirror, so somehow you traveled back through this mirror and opened the door for all of them then. They traveled through the tunnel, and you beat them through the mirror. You are like a princess who had the key to come back home."

I realized Rietje was talking about our previous journey traveling time to the seventeenth century which I wrote about in our diary *Entranced Beloved: I Shall Never Let You Go*. Emotionally for me, it was the hardest journey of my life as I left behind my beloved granddaughter Rietje and my wife Margriete of the seventeenth century had been buried. As I collapsed and returned unconscious, I was blessed to see my beloved Margriete in her new incarnation, with a completely different face. She was waiting for us to give all of us a second chance in life in the twenty-first century.

I sat down next to my two brothers who placed all the children on bean bags on the floor and took up the couches. Papa went back to my bed as did Mama. Margriete, Katelijne, and Tara Bella sat on the opposite couch, while Uncle Kees and Aunt Marinda sat on the love seat.

Uncle Kees gave Papa his glass as he had brought with him a glass of champagne. Papa sipped it slowly as if he was treasuring the drink. Mama gave him a stare and I knew he was going to be screamed at later.

Suddenly we saw both boys, Theunis and Alexander, become adults in front of our eyes. They could just change whenever they needed to. It was so strange and took a lot for us to get used to it. The wind never changes. The light and speed or anything never change, but the boys just become adults in a blink, as they wish.

Theunis got up and said, "When you all visited last time, I saw you would all be lost in the tunnel of light. Even in your sleep, if you travel at times, you get lost as someone must open the door from the other side. Margriete had passed away in front of a mirror that was left open. Her pure soul traveled to her current body through the mirror and reunited even though she was already born in the current time and had all her memories. Whoever opened the door for all of you, has a pure clean soul and is pure in heart."

Dawn was breaking through the skies in the Netherlands. I was having a hard time digesting everything. I didn't want to cloud any thoughts with my own thoughts. I wished I could have remembered everything that happened on the night my family members and I returned to Kasteel Vrederic in the twenty-first century after traveling back to the seventeenth century. We had left a crying Rietje, a newly wed bride, back in time.

It broke my heart to see her burying both me and her Oma Margriete. We were her only family members, her grandparents who raised her. Her mother Griet and her father Theunis had passed away and were the famous spirits of Kasteel Vrederic.

Theunis looked at me as I realized he read my mind and continued, "I had to give Margriete the keys I had with me as we all buried her, so she too would not be lost like Aunt Marinda and Succubus. Both were lost in a mirror as both died in front of a mirror which was left open for them to travel time. If you leave a mirror open when a person passes away, they can travel through the mirror."

I saw Margriete was shaken at the newfound information. She held Griet tightly in her embrace. It's always at these times our children become the adults. I told myself to be strong and not panic as things then only get worse.

Theunis spoke again as he knew I had stopped wandering off in my mind, "So, I had to find a way to make sure Margriete could be back through the time-traveling mirrors, as she would have the only keys to the portal of time. Aunt Marinda was good in heart, so she traveled with pure intention. Succubus was bad and evil, so she always traveled through dark doors. As Margriete died with the keys, she left an imprint of her face and hands on the mirror. So, she is the only one who opened the door for you all and can do it again as she wills or when you all must travel."

Alexander loved getting attention from Margriete. He grabbed orange juice and fruit salad from her as she was now feeding the children. I assumed she was hungry. When she is hungry, she makes sure the children are all fed even though they might not be hungry.

Alexander was munching as he said with food in his mouth, "Time traveling is hard. Only with a lot of courage and power can one travel. As Theunis explained, he himself had chosen Margriete to be the holder of the keys which also have the woman in the mirror sketch imprinted on them. It still baffles me how Theunis brought this mystical mirror in that small hidden chamber during the war. We had kept it there for you all to have a chance in another lifetime if needed."

Theunis and Alexander stood by one another as they spoke silently. Although nothing was said or heard, we knew they were buddies for centuries, and they could talk without uttering words. Theunis just nodded his head and glanced at Alexander. It was his way of saying continue with your words, I am with you, and I will help when you need my help.

Alexander continued, "After you all had left, we were worried what happened to all of you. Rietje cried and prayed for a miracle, so she could see or know if you were all right, or if the whole thing was just a dream. Theunis came back as the spirits of the lighthouse never left. He gave Rietje this mirror which she was advised to save in the same room. He told us we would all meet again. That's the only thing that Rietje had to hold and believe as she went on with her life without you, Jacobus and Margriete."

Alexander looked at Theunis and I realized Alexander wanted him to continue this time. It's amazing how I know these boys. I really feel like their father figure as I know how each one acts or would act. I admired both in my last life and am blessed to have them back in this lifetime as well.

Theunis said, "I told Rietje that Margriete had traveled and reincarnated. The mirror would bring Margriete to Kasteel Vrederic. I let her know that Margriete would be there when everyone returned and that Rietje too would be born from her grandmother's womb. I told her Margeriete would be her mother in the new life. Griet would become her cousin as again Margriete, the pure soul, would sacrifice her love and let another woman have Griet rather than lose her all over again. These were the only words my girl Rietje had to move on with."

I worried what was happening as I got even more confused. My baby girl Rietje jumped into my arms. She kissed my cheeks as Griet came running and kissed my cheeks at the same time. Their kisses always comforted me more than anything else in this world. I knew kisses from these two girls always removed all my worries. Actually, I taught them to kiss me as I kissed them from their birth. In our European household, we kiss to show our feelings.

I held both girls in my chest as Rietje said, "I knew you were all lost, so I prayed for a miracle. The one with the purest soul would be present at Kasteel Vrederic in your time of need. She is the woman in the mirror. If not for her, you all would have been prisoners in the tunnel of light. She would be there without even realizing, as the woman with pure intentions would help all of you then and all of us now without knowing. The woman with the keys had come to awaken everyone. So, she was Snow White, and you all were like Sleeping Beauty. Silly Papa, it was Mama always. She is the woman in the mirror, silly boy."

Margriete jumped up as she was more frightened at herself than she was at hearing this side of the story. I knew my wife and could tell she somehow knew about this. She had always said she kept dreaming we were all stuck somewhere and were knocking on an invisible door. She had opened the door in time, otherwise we all would have been lost in time.

Theunis said to Margriete, "You should have known. You gave me a home when I was a spirit without fearing me. You raised Alexander and me in this life without ever asking anything. You gave up Griet, your own daughter, so she could be reborn again in this home. You brought back Rietje as your child. Don't ever forget it was you who had opened the door for Jacobus and the whole family to return home and become immortal from the tunnel of light."

Theunis and Alexander both hugged Margriete. These boys are so close with her. In our last life, Margriete had taken care of all four of the children. She never questioned nor asked for anything but only loved my family members and me without asking for anything. She was almost burned alive at the gallows and still never feared nor asked for anything. She is the woman who gives and never asks for anything in return.

Theunis said, "You are the only person I saw and knew as my mother, not mother-in-law. As you became my life, I gave you the key to the tunnel of light to save your beloved family members as per your will. The woman in the mirror is the woman who was not born with powers. Aunt Marinda was born with time-traveling powers. Succubus was born as a demoness in a human body seeking other evil humans whom she could take over as they permitted her to do so. Incubus had known you are the woman in the mirror with the keys even though he didn't know about me."

Margriete was tearing up as she is very soft inside a hard shell. She was frightened at herself and held me tightly. Mama came and hugged her in her arms and kissed her head.

Mama told her "Dugga Dugga, remember all women have the power to protect their families. A woman can be a mother and protect her children from anything or anyone. A woman can become a snake and bite her enemies if one so must. Don't cry my child as God has made this miraculous mirror to save all of us through your blessed hands. My child, never question any miracle. Accept them as that's why they are just miracles."

Theunis walked to the fireplace and touched the mirror with his hands. The mirror was glowing and looked like a tunnel which was moving forward like a whirlwind.

In the tunnel, there was a woman who stood in the middle. It was Margriete from the seventeenth century. She examined all of us and then disappeared. I ran toward the tunnel as I thought was Margriete lost? Did she need any help? For some weird reason, I thought I could maybe help her, yet then I saw my own self holding her. It was as if they both saw us. I couldn't tell if they were seeing us or not.

Margriete turned to me with the same question in her eyes, if I was here or there. We both realized we were the same, one set belonged between the sixteenth and seventeenth centuries while the other set belonged in the twenty-first century.

Theunis laughed and said, "People go crazy when they travel time. Remember Margriete, you had kept Aunt Marinda and Uncle Kees alive by being here. For you, the members of the Kasteel Vrederic family are back here. Otherwise, that one night everyone would have been lost if only you had not opened the door by just being here. That's why Incubus also sought you by pretending to be Dr. Avyaan."

Papa and Mama were trying to understand what was happening as was everyone else. My question was how did Aunt Marinda, a time traveler, get trapped in a mirror? That's why she was always physically everywhere without ever being questioned about how, why, or where she came from. She didn't look like a ghost or a spirit, as she was a physical time traveler.

Margriete asked Theunis, "My child, I am so confused what's going on? I thought Aunt Marinda was the woman in the mirror, then I thought it was Succubus. How is it me when I was the only one who was initially mortal and only immortal as I married into this family? I'm still so confused."

Theunis kissed her head and hugged her in his arms. Alexander ran and copied Theunis as he too hugged her and kissed her head. They both sat on the floor next to her petite body near the couch. Theunis stood up and stared outside. We could all see the lagoon in our backyard.

He said, "Margriete you love fresh air, so you shall always have fresh air. You loved this home and so did Griet, Rietje, and Alexander, so we have all returned home to be with you, only you, the woman with the keys to my heart. Like Anadhi said, miracles are just that miracles."

Theunis stood in front of the windows for a long time as if was trying to think how he, a spiritual being, could explain everything to the human minds who are having a difficult time understanding everything. Again, without even moving from his spot next to Margriete, he just extended his arms and got himself a bottle of orange juice. Then, he adjusted the fire in the fireplace with his bare hands from across the room. We all saw he could do things beyond human capability, but no one said anything. We all know he is different as for centuries he had been roaming around as a spirit for his beloved Griet.

He then said to Margriete, "I gave you my own keys. I made the lighthouse on top of Kasteel Vrederic, only because remember Margriete, you had wished for one. With it, a mirror appeared and was hidden behind the fireplace in your room always. It was in the room where you had hidden with Jacobus, Rietje, and Alexander during the war. Like I said, a mirror can trap a soul if someone dies, and the mirror is left uncloaked at the time of death. Succubus killed Aunt Marinda in front of a mirror, and that's how she imprisoned Aunt Marinda. Succubus forgot Aunt Marinda is a time traveler, so Aunt Marinda went back to the time before her death and has been trying to get back to us. She was imprisoned by Succubus, but she survived because she is a time traveler."

The skies became clear outside the windows. The winter's cold air was coming inside the room. For some reason, the cold air woke all of us from a trance we had been transfixed into. I knew whatever happened, I had my family members all with me. Everything would be all right if we all stuck together and fought the unseen unknown enemies together.

Theunis glanced at me, and he gave me the same smile he had done centuries ago. I remember he had wounds on his body and was still so strong. I assume he heals differently than we humans do. Even though Theunis was in pain when I had met him in the sixteenth century, he still laughed and was jolly. He was a friend whom I was blessed to have had.

He said, "I had given Rietje this mirror and told her to hide it after Margriete had passed away in front of it. So, she can at any time, travel through it or help others through this mirror. I told Rietje to remember the mirror must be hidden away from all demons and demonesses, as they will try to find it. Remember Succubus is stuck in the sixteenth century as that's when she died and all mirrors to this century are blocked off."

Theunis touched this mirror with his bare hands. Neither did he move, nor did he say anything. He just touched the mirror which was across the room from him. He walked over there. We all tried not to blink our eyes or else we would miss the action. Andries stood up with his mouth open. Mama pulled him back to be quiet and listen. Theunis didn't miss our actions. He laughed out loud and winked toward Andries.

Theunis continued with his thoughts and told Margriete, "This mirror survived, and the sketch is not of the fairytale character Snow White, but the woman I have given the space of a mother in my heart. If you survey it carefully, you will see the sketch has your past life's face and this life's face engraved on it. It's a two-sided mirror."

I had seen this mirror and had always thought it was a painting, not a mirror. The mirror had on the bottom of it, a handprint that looked like a key. I am blessed Theunis had preplanned all our safety even from centuries ago. I had once upon a time called him my warrior, the protector of Kasteel Vrederic. I knew then and know now he is the protector of Kasteel Vrederic.

I asked Theunis, "I'm so confused. Now what happens with us and Alice the Succubus, and all the boys and girls who were killed by her? I understand souls get trapped in a mirror when they pass away. Succubus was dead and intended to be sucked into a mirror when she wanted to be released, but she needs a mirror to do so. I'm assuming it must be a special mirror. What about all the people she murdered? Were their souls sucked into mirrors too? How will we save them, or are their souls lost forever?"

Silence fell across the room as we all remembered how so many innocent lives had been taken. As doctors, Margriete and I had taken an oath to save lives every single day. It pained us to see we had landed in front of a demoness who thrived by taking lives.

Theunis just stood silent and then went close to the mirror. He said, "I am assuming that's why Incubus has shattered all the mirrors. So, all the souls would be lost and free. Succubus has left the body of Alice. Aunt Marinda and Uncle Kees would be fine in the present and the future. Never can they return to the past. They are both forever free of her if they never travel time to the past. We must try to stop them from traveling even if they insist, which they very likely will."

Theunis was walking back and forth as he touched his blond hair with his hands. The breeze was moving his long hair onto his eyes. He was thinking about something, and I saw for the first time, his blue eyes sparkled like glitter when he was thinking. I wondered if it was fire in his eyes. The glow that comes from the lighthouse is identical to whatever I just saw coming from his eyes. He saw me and laughed as he knew I just figured out how his eyes sparkle.

Theunis winked at me and continued, "The world, however, is thinking Alice the physical person is mental. She murdered innocent people through a demoness. If she was good, she could have said no. You must know that one must invite a demoness in to even be possessed. Remember, her hands committed the crimes, not the hands of Succubus. Succubus, the blood sucking demoness, has throughout time wiped away so many innocent lives. She separated true lovers for her own selfish needs which she did at times through other innocent humans. After Succubus does the job, they don't remember anything. As she is now finally imprisoned in the sixteenth century, we must make sure no one opens a mirror inviting her."

I was not getting what Theunis was leading us to as I was confused. Aunt Marinda, however, understood. She was a physical time traveler who never let us know what she had gone through but was always there for all of us.

She walked closer to Theunis and said, "So, everything is back to normal except for the people who lost their lives. What about Dr. Avyaan? Where is he now? Why is he not locked up in a time period, and why does he get to be free? I know he knew what his wife was doing yet he never stopped her. Theunis, remember, Succubus is a demoness. She has no heart. She will travel if you all are late."

Aunt Marinda was staring at everyone for a while. Then, she abruptly broke into tears. I saw her tears were falling. I wanted to run and wipe them off, but Margriete motioned me not to do so. I realized sometimes it was better to just let the tears fall.

Aunt Marinda said, "I am all right. I know I was lucky because I was able to travel time with my real physical body. Yet at times, I could stay days without anyone ever realizing I would have to be back in that cabin, or the mirror. I could travel freely even though Succubus imprisoned me by killing my physical body. I was still alive as I had the gift of eternal love which my husband, my twin flame, had given me. As Succubus killed me and separated my husband and me, we both got something of hers and became somewhat immortal like her."

I saw a very emotional Aunt Marinda. Mama went and held her as she knew Aunt Marinda needed someone to hold her and tell her everything would be all right. Mama without any words did that to all of us.

Aunt Marinda said, "I don't know how I became a time traveler like her, yes like the demoness. She tried to do evil, and I tried to do good and wipe away her evil doings. I always remembered she was my niece, well at least one of her physical bodies was. She escaped so many times as she was and to this day is still a demoness time traveler. I knew from the union of the two most powerful demons would be born my pure and most kind warrior, Theunis. I guess I held on as long as I could and so did Kees, until Theunis got his full powers. He would be the King of demons, not them. At that point, we would finally find justice."

Strangely, Theunis said nothing but looked toward his feet. Margriete did say something that shocked us all.

She said, "It's good Theunis was free to choose his own path and now my boy has all his powers because that's why I have my Theunis. He was born from the demonic world, but we have him because Incubus and his evil wife took over human bodies, like Alice's on Earth. Succubus seduced a man, but I guess Incubus took over the man who Succubus thought she seduced. It's weird and strange but who am I to question a demon and a demoness? Just leave my Theunis alone. I raised him then as my spiritual son-in-law and now as the father of Kasteel Vrederic, not just the lighthouse."

I worried how Margriete knew all of this, but I remembered she knew much more about Theunis and his truth from our last life which she never shared with anyone as Theunis was like our son not just son-in-law. Theunis had hinted at the truth of himself with Margriete in our past life.

I knew Margriete was talking but I kept getting lost in my own thoughts. I was worried about Margriete and wanted to protect her at any cost. Why did I feel like I have to keep an extra eye out for the innocent woman who never thinks about her own self?

I heard her say, "My daughter fell in love and changed him. She made him a human who loves and wants to only be good and do good. My daughter and my granddaughter turned a stone into a flower through simple love. I knew his secrets in my past life and even in this life. I will always protect them in my heart, as I want all of you to also protect Theunis and his secrets."

I admired how my wife spoke up for her son-in-law whom she adopted in her heart as a son. I realized this bond was from two lifetimes of love, not just one. I had loved him like my best friend as in my past life I had no friend other than Theunis.

Aunt Marinda kissed Theunis and said, "I would never change this part of history, but am scared to even change any part of history. What if we try to change the murdered victims to be alive, won't we play with history? Also, I will come with you if you are planning to go anywhere to get Succubus. I won't let you all risk your lives when I could be the only one who could see you all in the past and the future and not go crazy."

Margriete went to Aunt Marinda, held her in her arms, kissed her on the head, and said, "No with a capital N-O. You and Uncle Kees will be here to open the door if we get stuck again in the tunnel of light. I understand what Theunis is saying. We must travel to the sixteenth century when Succubus murdered Griet and tried to stop the family members of Kasteel Vrederic from even being in existence. She didn't know the same coffin Aunt Marinda's body was brought in was used to bring Griet's body who continued our dynasty even after death."

I finally got the pictures in my head clear as I had brought Griet's body back myself with Theunis's live body. He had buried himself in the same coffin with his wife as he said they would be together in life or in death. The coffin that had ripped so many hearts and kept all the secrets was buried in my family's *Evermore Beloved* garden.

I asked Theunis, "What's our next plan? We can live happily ever after if we don't ever go back in time as Succubus is trapped in the past. Or we can travel back in time to make sure she never hunts or taunts anyone else or tries to change our past over there."

We all heard a voice we were very familiar with now as he screamed and tried to be heard over a lot of static.

Dr. Avyaan the Incubus said, "I have traveled time to make sure Succubus in her past form never touches any of my son's bloodline. I will wait for you there as the war must continue so we can eternally wipe away the demoness known by various names across the world. We all know her as Succubus. Unfortunately, I had fallen madly in love with her until she betrayed me. Instead of walking away, I too betrayed our vows."

The sound stopped, but the static continued. My brothers were trying to find out where the sound was coming from. Antonius and Andries walked around the room trying to find the sound box. They stomped their feet in anger yet were lost as we all were, thinking how he just entered our home. We did, however, again hear the deep scratchy voice.

He said, "Ahh don't search for me or where and how you hear my voice, as you will never find me unless I want to be found. Don't rush. We will always be here in this time period, but again I warn you not to delay. Also, I had kept one surprise from you Jacobus. Are you thinking what? Hmm, we met in the past Jacobus as I am the fisherman who had tried to give you, your daughter."

I jumped up at those words. That was the gravest mistake of my life. I live with the mistake of sending away my own child. Only a cold and bitter person could do that, yet I had done exactly that.

Incubus laughed out loud as he continued and said, "Well, I tried to be nice and save her. I didn't know, however, she wouldn't need my saving as she would marry my son the King of demons. Your arrogance and Erasmus's anger problems contributed to all this mess. Come back and only change the fate of Succubus the demoness, not anyone else's. Make sure you don't change anyone else's fate. Just find the Succubus who has traveled time, not the one who was here originally. I will travel again if I have to, but remember, I am already there in the fisherman's body."

We then heard a laughter fade away as if someone was traveling away from our home. My brothers and I were confused how we would travel time again, and if it was safe to do it all over again. For now, we decided we would take our time as we had in our hands the only portal to travel time, the mirror. We also had the woman in the mirror with us as she is the only holder of the key to travel time if we needed to.

Aunt Marinda and Uncle Kees both kissed Margriete as Aunt Marinda said, "You were always the woman in the mirror, the holder of the time-traveling keys. I was born as a time traveler, so I could do it to help my family members only. You earned the mirror and the key through your eternal love for your husband and family members. You were the only one who knew Theunis's secrets and never told anyone as you even took his secret to your grave with you. The son you never had was your son-in-law, who loved you more than anyone else on or beyond this world, the one who is a man and King of the demonic world, Theunis Peters. The only remaining mirror with Margriete's face was created by Theunis as a time-traveling tunnel. This mirror has been for centuries linked to mysterious things."

Mama got up and opened all the curtains. She busied herself in getting light poured into the house. My mother believes in vampires and thinks only good vampires can stand the light and all evil can't stand the light poured onto Earth through the biggest star in our solar system, the Sun.

Mama said to everyone, "Well, let's have Marinda and Kees retake their wedding vows. A small breakfast event, like a breakfast wedding. Then, let's enjoy the days we all have until we must travel time again. Like I said last time, it doesn't matter if we are in this period or another, we have each other and that's all I want. The Kasteel Vrederic family members will always be together in whichever period we end up. We're not afraid of any mirrors or tunnels as we're only scared of having hungry boys in our home."

Theunis became a child again as did Alexander. They both went to Mama, and I knew the boys were hungry. I didn't know what to do but realized today we wouldn't decide on anything as today we were all happy to know Succubus was stuck in the past. The people in the streets of London and around the world were safer. Yes, we lost a lot of innocent women and men who died for an evil woman's exotic unrequited desires.

I saw the mirror on top of our wall was glowing and the sketch of the woman was becoming clearer. She looked like a picture of my Margriete. We all saw Margriete inspect the mirror herself. I knew she was frightened as she had to decide what we should do. She just held on to Mama's hands as I knew she found comfort within my mother's embrace.

Griet knew Margriete was worried, so she went up to her and held her hand as she said, "Don't rush. You will know when and which date we must travel. The door won't open before or after. The mirror will make sure everyone who needs to travel with us are all here when it opens the door at your touch. The mirror is double sided so when you reach your destination, it will close the door and open again when you must return."

Margriete held Griet in her embrace. For a long time, nothing was said or heard as the two just embraced one another.

Margriete said, "My baby girl, once upon a time I prayed under the twinkling stars to just hold you for even one more minute in my embrace. Today I have you, so I won't let a minute go to waste. When I can hug you, I will. It's like a thirst I had that needed to be quenched. I won't rush or be scared as in this life, I have you by my side."

The atmosphere in the room was very emotional. Every single member of this household wanted to be there for Griet. I was not there for her in our past life but will be there for her eternally as she will always be a part of my inner soul. My brothers realized we needed a break and always in their own ways made things better even on heavy days.

My two brothers were laughing as they questioned whose tummy had grumbled. They were blaming each other as I heard both tummies were grumbling.

Now like a competition, they both said, "Breakfast time! We're hungry Big Mama. Aunt Marinda and Uncle Kees, come on, retake your vows! Jacobus can help. He was a preacher in his last life."

Suddenly Antonius peeked at the mirror. He stopped in place and talked out loud, like he always does.

Antonius said, "So funny, the only mirror with the woman was in front of our eyes. We had collected so many mirrors, the one from Malibu where Aunt Marinda was, then the other one, the medallion which too was a mirror that imprisoned Succubus. How is it we all missed our own mirror on the wall? It was always here, and I always wondered how Margriete's face was in it. You know, I thought it was a painting which looked like a mirror but actually was not."

Margriete seemed content as she saw Aunt Marinda and Uncle Kees and said, "I am happy I don't have to decide when or who I must take with me as the mirror will decide for all of us. Oh boy, I feel like a huge burden has just been lifted from my chest."

It didn't surprise me. She wasn't frightened to travel time but whether she would offend anyone by not taking them or leaving anyone behind. I knew how innocent she was and why Theunis loved her so much as he gave her the only key to his own world and beyond, the only bridge that connects every world, and was a time-traveling device. This mirror can disappear and appear at its own will. At times, it's there on the wall, then again at times, it's not there at all.

All the mirrors around the world broke, but everyone just thought it was an unexplainable phenomenon of the world we lived in. This mirror never broke, never shook, and never even tilted as this is a magical mirror where lived the eternally beloved, the evermore beloved, my twin flame, the woman who had with her love created the lover's lighthouse. She had Theunis place it on top of our home in the sixteenth century.

Throughout time, people would see the beloved twin flames kissing inside of it. People had thought if they saw the kissing twin flames, then their twin flame was standing next to them. My family members including myself had sought guidance from this magical lighthouse. Margriete had known this lighthouse would throughout time protect our descendants as it did protect our ancestors.

Unlike all others we had rescued, Margriete was the one and only person never imprisoned or forced to be in any mirror even though she had died in front of one. She was the one the father of Kasteel Vrederic's lighthouse trusted. He gave her the only keys that opened the time tunnel hidden in the blessed mirror that had a sketch of Margriete, the blessed woman in the mirror.

WOMAN IN THE MIRROR

Pure and innocent souls

Are never trapped,

As the paranormal world says.

After death,

The bodies get trapped

In a mirror

If it is not covered.

Yet what about

The woman who guides

From within a mirror?

What about the mother,

The grandmother,

The pious, and

The righteous woman

Who gives up

Everything

To only love

And protect

Her family members?

What about the one

Who sacrifices

All she has

Or all her needs

To be with her beloved

In this life

Or beyond?

She says

She will protect her beloved

From near or far.

She is always there

For him

As he is always there for her.

Throughout time

And through

All incarnations,

She will use the door

Of a mirror to only

Protect,

Preserve, and

Honor

The pure sanctuaries

Of true love

Forever.

The door of a mirror

Shall guide her

The purest,

The honorable, and

The beloved

To travel time and tide

To be where and when

She is needed.

She is the only one,

The one and only,

WOMAN IN THE MIRROR.

CONCLUSION:

BRIDE OF THE IMMORTAL

"Fear grips
The inner soul,
Yet it also warns us
Danger is
Looming around."

The Kasteel Vrederic household was celebrating a newlywed couple. We had traveled to New Orleans, Louisiana in the USA, as Aunt Marinda before becoming completely human had traveled through time over there. We asked her to limit her time traveling only to the present and future, not ever to the past.

Visiting New Orleans was a very emotionally draining experience. We visited a friend who was discriminated against through ageism. Also, my mother and father had only recently adopted a friend of my brothers Antonius and Andries as their son. It's actually very hard to adopt a grown-up son, but somehow, Mama and Papa were able to go through the red tapes. We brought him home after a very emotional and paranormal trip. You can read about this emotional journey in *The Bride, The Groom, And The Ghost*.

Mama was very emotional as we buried him in our *Evermore Beloved* garden. Yes, our adopted brother passed away before my parents could give him the adoption papers. My family says he just left his old broken-down vehicle and now is ready with his brand-new vehicle to come back to Earth.

Sunday brunch in the Kasteel Vrederic household was always filled with laughter and joy. We placed all our sorrows under the pillows where we buried our tears and greeted the new promising dawn.

The table was filled with foods from around the globe. Katelijne made Italian sfogliatella. Tara Bella made Indian samosas. Margriete made aloo parathas. Mama made pannenkoeken and hagelslag. Aunt Marinda made her favorite American breakfast with scrambled eggs, toast, and fresh brewed coffee. Papa, Uncle Kees, Antonius, Andries, and I made masala dosa.

The table was full, and everyone helped themselves to whatever their hearts desired. I knew we were all dreading the subject of when we would be asked or shown it's time to travel. This travel was not just hop on an airplane and only hope you don't get jet lag. The mirror on top of our fireplace remained calm and had not shown any sign of wanting to open the door of time traveling to us. We had taken the mirror with us even to New Orleans thinking what if we must travel.

Our newlywed couple celebrated their wedded bliss quietly in a small cottage on the Kasteel Vrederic property. The same cottage once upon a time was our carriage house, the house Margriete and I had united in during the sixteenth century. The couple wanted to be close to us but wanted some space. So, the small cottage became their home.

Aunt Marinda said, "Jacobus, I got a call from Dr. Avyaan this morning. He said all the women who were murdered by Succubus don't exist anymore as if the whole events surrounding Succubus never happened. Then, the family members who came from them too would not exist. He said this is very dangerous. He also said he can't travel time as all the portals are closed. So, we must decide what to do."

I was horrified how did he even get Aunt Marinda's contact information. All her information was private. I didn't ask as I knew he could get in touch if he so wanted to.

Theunis answered my unasked questions, "He has ways to get in touch with anyone he so wishes to be in touch with. He tried to go back in time again but found out he can't as he is stuck in this time period only. He can't go to the future either. If he does anything bad, he found out he would become nothing but just dust. Like a vampire, he would become ashes not because of the sun but if he travels time. So, he tries to keep himself busy, trying to find miracle cures for the humans and himself as he too is a human now or maybe like a vampire."

Antonius laughed out loud as he and Andries both almost choked on their food. Mama told them to be quiet without uttering the words.

Antonius, however, said, "It's funny Big Mama. It's like the only way to get some good out of the evil. He is helping cure humans as he needs the same cure for himself."

It felt good to know maybe this world would get more needed cures soon. I knew because Incubus had supernatural powers, we would definitely discover new treatments.

Then suddenly out of the blue, I had a cold feeling that something wasn't right. It felt as if time was running out and I could almost see an hourglass emptying out quickly. The riddle had never been solved as to why we were not being sent back in time, or who decides as I knew my wife was scared to make the decision.

As a doctor, she makes decisions, but not when so many people's fates are involved, and the outcomes are not even in sight or ever proven to be safe.

Griet was suddenly crying as she kept saying, "It hurts! It hurts!"

I ran to her as did her biological father Antonius and everyone else.

She cried again as she looked at Antonius and again said, "Theunis, I don't want to die without knowing who or where Papa is. Please find him. I need to see him at least once. I just want to say, even though his cold heart doesn't beat my name, my heart still seeks his love and answers to why he never accepted me."

I froze in my own space as I knew she was talking about my ruthless past. I was a heartless person, or at least that's what everyone assumed. How could I tell a person hurting so much, I never stopped looking after one dreadful mistake. I had searched for her all her living life and only found her when her heart beats stopped calling out for me.

My heart beats called out for her eternally. I wondered what would have happened if I could have been there before her death? Could I travel in time and save my child? Or would I then change everyone's fate? Margriete then grabbed Griet as did her biological mother Katelijne.

Margriete said with tears pouring from her eyes, "Theunis, please help her. She lived for you and died becoming your wife while trying to save her own daughter. Please don't let her feel the pain from her last life."

Griet stood up on her feet as Rietje touched her and said, "No pain okay. I am here. I am the daughter of the immortal, so you are the bride of the immortal."

Margriete's hands began to light up as did Aunt Marinda's. We knew these were signs of our impending time-travel mission.

Aunt Marinda said, "She knows we are coming for she awaits our arrival. We must be careful when and how we travel. We can't let our past selves see us. We can't interfere with our past selves. Somehow, we must make sure the evil demoness who wanted to be the woman in the mirror, who had imprisoned me as the woman in the mirror, is confronted by the real woman in the mirror."

Uncle Kees and Aunt Marinda held one another as they smiled happily to be together.

They both said, "Let's travel time. I think it's time this family takes a journey together. All for one, one for all."

Theunis held Griet and checked her head. He was worried but he smiled and hugged Rietje.

Theunis said, "We have the original and only woman in the mirror with the keys to the time-traveling tunnels with us. Aunt Marinda and Uncle Kees are united and shall never again face any separation, through time or space. Aunt Marinda is free from being imprisoned in the mirror by force or hiding in it to be safe, be it her own choice to travel, or through the hands of an evil demoness. Succubus can never travel through the tunnel of light or any mirrors, but she will try. We must rush."

I saw Mama was getting things cleared up from the table as she poured herself a cup of tea. She poured Papa a cup of coffee and then offered everyone coffee and tea of their choice.

Mama laughed and said, "Jacobus, the diary of the woman in the mirror is finished because you have rescued Aunt Marinda from the Stonehenge and Uncle Kees from being a prisoner in a sarcophagus in the pyramids of Giza. You have also found the identity of our blessed woman in the mirror. Now we must end the demoness, her time traveling, and stop her from placing any more prisoners in mirrors, sarcophagi, or any huts."

I hugged Aunt Marinda and Uncle Kees and told them, "You two must stay here. Get caught up on everything you two have missed over the years. Keep an eye out on Kasteel Vrederic as we will travel time again to protect and preserve our family's honor and grace."

I smiled and saw how ready my family members were. Aunt Marinda stomped her feet as she walked around the table cleaning up the dishes.

She then stopped and looked me directly in the eyes as she said, "As you are my nephew whom I consider to be like a son, you listen to me. Whatever the risks may be, I will not sit here and wait for good or bad news to come to me, when I could be with my beloved family members. At any cost, be it dead or alive, do you really think I will still be alive after worrying if you all are going to make it back or not?"

We had all been drained out trying to get our business in order all day. If we were going to be stuck in time, we didn't want the world to question where we were. We called Bertelmeeus to come and stay at the house and realized he too came prepared to travel with us, not stay away from us.

The night's singing birds were all singing sweet songs as my family members all hung around Margriete's and my bedroom chamber. We knew we were all ready to travel time and meet the lovebirds of times past. This time, we would be traveling through the help of the woman in the mirror to the land of the immortal and his bride.

You all can read what happens next as I will pen onto paper another diary of the Kasteel Vrederic library which we call *Bride Of The Immortal*.

BRIDE OF THE IMMORTAL

You the daughter

Found your belonging,

As you became a bride.

For as an orphan

You had survived,

Without any protection

From any

Helping hands.

As you were lost

And traveled alone,

You were found

Only by your beloved,

Your twin flame,

Who came and held you

Within his blessed chest,

To be safe,

To be guarded,

To be loved,

And never be lonely,

Ever again.

Yet

As you are a mortal,

And your beloved is

But immortal,

He chose to be with you,

Even in the grave,

Beyond this Earth,

Or above,

To reawaken

Again,

And again

As twin flames,

Oh,

You the beloved,

BRIDE OF THE IMMORTAL.

INHABITANTS OF
WOMAN IN THE MIRROR

Dr. Jacobus Vrederic van Phillip Medical doctor with multiple specialties, and one-of-a-kind specialist in never-done-before transplant surgeries. Son of Erasmus van Phillip and Anadhi Newhouse van Phillip, cousin of Antonius van Phillip and Andries van Phillip, uncle of reincarnated Andries van Phillip and Griet Vrederic van Phillip, twin flame and husband of Dr. Margriete van Achthoven van Phillip, and father of Rietje Vrederic van Phillip. Reincarnated form of sixteenth and seventeenth-century Jacobus van Vrederic.

Dr. Margriete van Achthoven van Phillip Medical doctor, cardiologist, and pediatric cardiovascular surgeon. Co-owner of Agatha and Marinda's Orphanage. Twin flame and wife of Dr. Jacobus Vrederic van Phillip, and mother of Rietje Vrederic van Phillip. Reincarnated form of sixteenth and seventeenth-century Margriete van Wijck.

Anadhi Newhouse van Phillip Author. Daughter of Dr. Andrew Newhouse and Dr. Gita Shankar Newhouse, granddaughter of Martin Newhouse and Miranda Newhouse, granddaughter of Hari Shankar and Parvati Shankar, twin flame and wife of Erasmus van Phillip, mother of Dr. Jacobus Vrederic van Phillip, aunt and adoptive mother of Antonius van Phillip and Andries van Phillip, grandmother of reincarnated Andries van Phillip, Griet Vrederic van Phillip, and Rietje Vrederic van Phillip. Reincarnated form of sixteenth-century Mahalt.

Erasmus van Phillip World-renowned painter, and twenty-first-century owner of Kasteel Vrederic. Son of Greta van Phillip, descendant of the Van Vrederic family, twin flame and husband of Anadhi Newhouse van Phillip, father of Dr. Jacobus Vrederic van Phillip, uncle and adoptive father of Antonius van Phillip and Andries van Phillip, and grandfather of reincarnated Andries van Phillip, Griet Vrederic van Phillip, and

Rietje Vrederic van Phillip. Reincarnated form of sixteenth-century Johannes van Vrederic.

Antonius van Phillip   World-renowned painter. Son of Petrus van Phillip and Giada Berlusconi van Phillip, nephew and adopted son of Erasmus van Phillip and Anadhi Newhouse van Phillip, twin brother of Andries van Phillip, cousin and adoptive brother of Dr. Jacobus Vrederic van Phillip, twin flame and husband of Katelijne Snaaijer van Phillip, and father of reincarnated Andries van Phillip and Griet Vrederic van Phillip.

Katelijne Snaaijer van Phillip   Stepdaughter of Ghileyn Snaaijer, twin flame and wife of Antonius van Phillip, and mother of reincarnated Andries van Phillip and Griet Vrederic van Phillip.

Andries van Phillip   Deceased world-renowned pianist, son of Petrus van Phillip and Giada Berlusconi van Phillip, nephew and adopted son of Erasmus van Phillip and Anadhi Newhouse van Phillip, twin brother of Antonius van Phillip, and

cousin and adoptive brother of
Dr. Jacobus Vrederic van
Phillip. Now reincarnated son
of Antonius van Phillip and
Katelijne Snaaijer van Phillip,
grandson of Erasmus van
Phillip and Anadhi Newhouse
van Phillip, nephew of Dr.
Jacobus Vrederic van Phillip
and Dr. Margriete van
Achthoven van Phillip,
brother of Griet Vrederic van
Phillip, cousin of Rietje
Vrederic van Phillip, twin
flame and husband of Tara
Bella, and adoptive father of
Hana Bella van Phillip and
Ahana Bella van Phillip.

Tara Bella van Phillip Daughter of Sitara Bella and
Marcello Esposito, twin flame
and wife of Andries van
Phillip, and adoptive mother
of Hana Bella van Phillip and
Ahana Bella van Phillip.

Griet Vrederic van Daughter of Antonius van
Phillip Phillip and Katelijne Snaaijer
van Phillip, granddaughter of
Erasmus van Phillip and
Anadhi Newhouse van
Phillip, niece of Dr. Jacobus
Vrederic van Phillip and Dr.
Margriete Achthoven, sister
of Andries van Phillip, and
cousin of Rietje Vrederic van

Phillip. Reincarnated form of sixteenth-century Griet van Jacobus.

Rietje Vrederic van Phillip Daughter of Dr. Jacobus Vrederic van Phillip and Dr. Margriete van Achthoven, granddaughter of Erasmus van Phillip and Anadhi Newhouse van Phillip, and cousin of Andries van Phillip and Griet Vrederic van Phillip. Reincarnated form of sixteenth and seventeenth-century Margriete "Rietje" Jacobus Peters.

Theunis Peters Adopted son of Aunt Marinda. Adoptive brother of Alexander. Biological son of Incubus and Succubus. Reincarnated form of sixteenth-century Theunis Peters.

Alexander van der Bijl Adopted son of Aunt Marinda. Adoptive brother of Theunis. Reincarnated form of sixteenth and seventeenth-century Sir Alexander van der Bijl. Cousin of seventeenth-century Frederic van der Bijl.

Marinda van Vrederic Time traveler, spiritual seer, nurse, and herbalist from the sixteenth century in the present day. Co-owner of

Agatha and Marinda's
Orphanage. Sister of Agatha
and Tabitha, adoptive
guardian of Theunis and
Alexander, and twin flame
and wife of Kees van
Vrederic.

Kees van Vrederic   Son of Marinus van Vrederic
and Sakina, brother of
Johannes van Vrederic, and
twin flame and husband of
Marinda.

Daemon the Incubus   Demon, husband of Succubus,
and biological father of
Theunis Peters.

Dr. Hans Avyaan   London-based doctor and
human form of Incubus in
twenty-first century.

Succubus   Demoness, wife of Incubus,
and biological mother of
Theunis Peters.

Alice   Teenage girl living in London
possessed by Succubus.

Bertelmeeus   Famous voluntary chef at the
Agatha and Marinda's
Orphanage and at the
Vrederic Hospital and Clinic,
and policeman. Reincarnated
form of sixteenth and

seventeenth-century
Bertelmeeus van der Berg.

Ahana Roy Child bride, and birth mother
of Hana Bella van Phillip and
Ahana Bella van Phillip.
Reincarnated form of
seventeenth-century Ahana
and twin flame of Frederic
van der Bijl.

Ahana Bella van Phillip Biological daughter of Ahana
Roy, sister of Hana Bella van
Phillip, and adopted daughter
of Andries van Phillip and
Tara Bella van Phillip.

Hana Bella van Phillip Biological daughter of Ahana
Roy, sister of Ahana Bella
van Phillip, and adopted
daughter of Andries van
Phillip and Tara Bella van
Phillip.

Dr. Noah Smith London-based doctor and
pyramidologist with expertise
on the pyramids of Giza.

Dr. Akins Ahmed A paranormal doctor sent by
Dr. Hans Avyaan.

GLOSSARY

Get acquainted with some Dutch and Hindi terms, and places in the Netherlands, the United Kingdom, the United States, and Egypt that were used in this book.

Ageism   Discrimination against an individual based on age.

Aloo Paratha   Indian flatbread stuffed with potatoes.

Amesbury   Name of a city and a parish in England.

Amsterdam Airport Schiphol   One of the busiest airports in the world and main international airport in the Netherlands.

Death   End of life on Earth, when the body and soul separate. More information on death can be found in the book *Eternal Truth: The Tunnel Of Light* by Ann Marie Ruby.

Demon   Male evil being.

Demoness   Female evil being.

Dream Psychic   One who sees past, present, and future through dreams.

Dreams REM (rapid eye movement) cycle is when a sleeping body can travel through dreams. Proven scientifically dreams can occur and people do travel during their dreams. However, their bodies do not leave their places. Major religions have mainly come through dreams. More information on dreams can be found in the book *Eternal Truth: The Tunnel Of Light* by Ann Marie Ruby.

Dugga Dugga Bengali phrase calling upon the Hindu Mother Goddess Durga.

Dutch Term refers to both the language spoken and the people in the Netherlands.

Egypt Country in Northern Africa.

England Country in Europe.

Evermore Beloved Garden Family graveyard in the *Kasteel Vrederic* series.

Gallows A place commonly known where witches were hung to their death.

Giza City in Egypt and home to famous ancient monuments

including the pyramids of Giza.

Great Pyramid Of Giza The largest pyramid in Egypt, one of the Seven Wonders of the World, and UNESCO World Heritage site.

Hagelslag Chocolate sprinkles.

Kasteel Vrederic Castle Vrederic is the home of the Van Vrederic/Van Phillip family in the *Kasteel Vrederic* series, spanning from the sixteenth century through the present.

London Capital of England and the United Kingdom.

Malibu A famous beach city in California.

Masala Dosa Indian crispy crepe usually made with rice and lentil batter.

Miracles Unexpected gift that cannot be explained by science or medicine. More information on miracles can be found in the book *Eternal Truth: The Tunnel Of Light* by Ann Marie Ruby.

Naarden   City in the province of North Holland in the Netherlands.

New Orleans   City and parish along the Mississippi River in Louisiana, nicknamed "The Big Easy."

New York City   Most populated city in the United States within the state of New York. The city includes the borough of Manhattan and is known as the "Big Apple."

Oma   Grandmother in Dutch.

Opa   Grandfather in Dutch.

Pannenkoeken   Dutch pancake.

Pyramidologist   Person who studies pyramids from a religious or supernatural stance.

Pyramids Of Giza   Several pyramids are in Giza, but there are three main pyramids which are the Pyramid of Menkaure, Pyramid of Khafre, and the Great Pyramid of Giza.

Reincarnation/Rebirth   Belief of a lot of people worldwide such as Buddhism, Hinduism, Jainism, Sikhism, and more. Today science can't disprove reincarnation. Also a lot of people have given proof of their rebirth. More information on reincarnation can be found in the book *Eternal Truth: The Tunnel Of Light* by Ann Marie Ruby.

Samosa   Popular fried Indian pastry filled with different things such as potatoes and vegetables.

Salisbury Plain   Located in Southern England, the Stonehenge is located here.

Sarcophagus   Ancient coffin boxes made out of stone where mummies were buried.

Sfogliatella   Italian pastry with a cream filling.

Sleep Paralysis   A stage that happens to a huge population of people around the globe. There is no research as to why it happens yet its existence is proven mythologically and scientifically.

Stakes   A place where witches were burned to death.

Stonehenge   Prehistoric monument made of stones located in the Salisbury Plain in England, and a

UNESCO World Heritage Site.

The Netherlands   Country in Western Europe.

The United Kingdom   Country in Northwestern Europe including England, Northern Ireland, Wales, and Scotland.

The United States   Country in North America.

Tunnel Of Light   Scientifically it is known as the NDE (near-death experience) tunnel. More information on the tunnel of light can be found in the book *Eternal Truth: The Tunnel Of Light* by Ann Marie Ruby.

Twin Flames   Research has shown twin flames can survive as individuals yet are complete in union. More information on twin flames can be found in the book *Eternal Truth: The Tunnel Of Light* by Ann Marie Ruby.

Vayu   Hindu God of wind, also known as Pavana and Vata.

MESSAGE FROM THE AUTHOR

"Fear incarcerates
The basic thinking aptitudes,
Yet if you could only let go
Of the fear facet,
Not holding on to
Your breath,
But taking slow and deep breaths,
You will know,
In a war where we fight,
Good versus evil, the
Virtuous is always victorious."

Dear Readers,

Good versus evil is a phenomenon humans have known from the beginning of time. If only Eve had not fallen for the apple. Some might say temptation is pure evil. Yet how do we fight evil? Is there any human power that can fight the known or unknown evil out there? What about our minds? Could evil control our minds?

Why would we fight destiny and not work with it? Eve had the apple, so we are all here on Earth. Let's not repeat what Eve did and learn from her mistakes. I say fight temptations. Fight evil with good from the bottom of your heart. How long could a person hate you or do evil onto you if you close the door and don't allow the person or their words to touch you? Stop evil at the door. Just remember not to open the door to the knocks of evil.

Evil comes and take shelter in the minds of pure evil. Evil beings have no power to control you, your minds, bodies, or souls. There are no ghosts, unrequited souls, or demons on Earth that are more powerful than you, your mind, and your soul. Close the door to them through your mind, and just watch them disappear. The most powerful creation on Earth are we the humans, so never fear any evil where you and I the good will always defeat evil with good.

Be it nonfiction or fiction, I always weave all my books with a hidden message. Here the message is not to fear the evil. By fearing the evil, we give them power. It's like we give them a free rechargeable generator. Why not give yourselves a free generator and overpower them by saying we fear no evil? They hide in the dark and we are out in the light. Who then has the more powerful generator? Obviously, we do.

This book is one such paranormal story where we see love is victorious. Love traveled time even when the lovers were no more. Love never dies for the story the lovers wrote found a home in the library of Kasteel Vrederic. No fear can detain the family members of Kasteel Vrederic. Fear is the only evil this world has given birth to.

Remember on the flip side, however, fear is also the only warning sign our inner soul gives us when danger is looming around the corner. Take your inner fears and make them the shields of your protection. It's simple when something unwanted comes close to your eyes, you and I close our eyes to keep them safe and protect our eyes from all harm. It's the fear in our souls that protects us.

In this book, I have weaved a love story that never found its ending. The story shattered like a broken mirror, as the lovers fell upon the evil eyes of a demoness. Yet, the pure and blessed love story crossed time and tide to awaken and let the world know, you can separate lovers, you can eliminate them from this Earth, but their love lives on. How could a bridge created by evil eyes break or wipe away a bridge created through love from inner souls?

Through a mirror from the beyond, a love story had begun and broken apart. The mirror brings back the lovers to only retell the story evil tried to bury through the same mirror. Little did the evil or the lovers know, all along they were being watched by the blessed woman in the mirror with her keys. Little did anyone know, all along this mirror was being protected by a key holder of the mirror chosen by the creator of the mirror. The holder of the keys is a pure soul who would never give in to the temptations of evil. I believe the good and pure souls are chosen by the supernatural as the protectors of all.

My message from this book is simple, believe in the power of good. Nothing in this world or beyond is more powerful than the simple truth of the mind which is the power of good.

In this time and place where we the humans have landed upon, people are fighting good and bad within the society, the country, and the world. The first step to eradicating all evil is eradicating it from oneself. Why give the power to anything bad in this world? Power yourselves up today with the simple truth, good.

Befriend your mind and you befriend your worst, for your enemy is gone because there's only one friend and that's your best friend, your own mind. If you are fighting with your mind and creating your own enemy, the worst enemy a human can have is your own mind.

Learn to befriend your mind, then erase the bad enemies you have created and only draw the good within your mind, body, and soul. You will see then you have become a complete individual. Once you have won this war and have become victorious between the bad and the good, you will become the complete individual who you were born to be.

One can control his own destiny for your destiny is in your mind. Remember if your mind creates a mountain of obstacles, then close your eyes and remove the mountain. Open your eyes and be free from all obstacles. Be free from all stress and rejuvenate from within.

Not all the obstacles in your path will be easy to remove, but never give up. Things will become clear as you wait it out. The dark nights will come but in between dark and dawn, let go of your worst enemy from your mind. Then, the obstacles you had will slowly evaporate. So what if some obstacles remain? You are stronger and you can remove them like stones, one at a time.

The Kasteel Vrederic family members united Aunt Marinda and Uncle Kees, which they knew they had to do. They know they still have more work in store for them which they know they will do one at a time. Just like I must write one book at a time, you all must take one step at a time.

Don't fear death. Don't fear demons or demonesses as you the human will reincarnate with faith. You will get over your fears as there are no monsters under the bed. No ghosts or demons can ever enter a house where there is faith in the Creator and His humans. You are the most powerful creation in this universe, so you can also resolve all your troubles. You the human can build a bridge over your troubles, but you need to remember to lay one brick at a time.

Now go and look into the mirror and see the most powerful human in the world is the face you see in the mirror.

Sending my love and blessings.

BOOK ONE:

Eternally Beloved: I Shall Never Let You Go
This book introduces you to Kasteel Vrederic through the first diary of the famous diarist Jacobus van Vrederic. He walks you through his sad love story and goes through the love story of his daughter Griet van Jacobus and the brave soldier Theunis Peter. Based during the Dutch Eighty Years' War in the sixteenth century.

BOOK TWO:

Evermore Beloved: I Shall Never Let You Go
Here you walk through the amazing love story of Jacobus van Vrederic and his beloved wife Margriete van Wijck, where we get to meet Jacobus's beloved granddaughter, baby Rietje. Based during the witch trials and the Dutch Eighty Years' War in the sixteenth and seventeenth centuries.

BOOK THREE:

Be My Destiny: Vows From The Beyond

This book takes you through reincarnation and the blessed door of dreams. Here infinite twin flames Erasmus van Phillip, a twenty-first-century descendant of Jacobus van Vrederic and the reincarnated father of Jacobus van Vrederic, is reborn again to find and unite with his forever twin flame, Anadhi Newhouse, also the reincarnated mother of Jacobus van Vrederic. Find out how their son reunites them through the twenty-first century and takes them back to Kasteel Vrederic.

BOOK FOUR:

Heart Beats Your Name: Vows From The Beyond

Here you will get introduced to a blind son of the Kasteel Vrederic family, the nephew and adopted son of Erasmus van Phillip and Anadhi Newhouse van Phillip. In this paranormal thriller, you will see how Dr. Jacobus Vrederic van Phillip, the biological son of Erasmus and Anadhi, guides his

297

brother to unite with his pronounced dead wife, while trying to solve her murder mystery. A paranormal book where everyone realizes family members are bound with one another throughout time.

BOOK FIVE:

Entranced Beloved: I Shall Never Let You Go

Twenty-first-century Dr. Jacobus Vrederic van Phillip must return to the seventeenth-century Kasteel Vrederic, as he realizes his beloved granddaughter is missing and must be rescued for the inhabitants of *Vows From The Beyond* to even exist. This can only be done through the miraculous hands of the famous twenty-first-century physician. So here we go, Dr. Jacobus must travel time and go back to the *I Shall Never Let You Go* diaries. Walk back and get reacquainted with the seventeenth-century Kasteel Vrederic family members with Dr. Jacobus as he meets his sixteenth-century self, Jacobus van Vrederic. Margriete "Rietje" Jacobus Peters and Sir Alexander van der Bijl's love story is written and retold by the twenty-first-century famous physician, Dr. Jacobus from the *Vows From The Beyond* diaries.

BOOK SIX:

Forbidden Daughter Of Kasteel Vrederic: Vows From The Beyond

Dr. Jacobus Vrederic van Phillip and Dr. Margriete van Achthoven through the door of reincarnation traveled time yet now must face the wagon of karma. The unborn child asks, "Why am I the forbidden daughter of Kasteel Vrederic?" With the answer, revolves the existence of the Kasteel Vrederic Lover's Lighthouse and the father of the lighthouse. Trying to find an answer to this question, Dr. Jacobus finds out his family is being terrorized by a murderer who hides within Kasteel Vrederic.

BOOK SEVEN:

The Immortality Serum: Vows From The Beyond

A woman in red walks around the Newhouse Castle calling on everyone to get out as the house was on fire. What she did not know was everyone in the house was still with the living yet she, the woman in red, was the only one dead. Andries van Phillip calls upon his twin flame Tara Bella, the woman in red, to awaken and walk out of her glass coffin. The Kasteel Vrederic family members travel from the Netherlands to Malibu, California to rescue Tara Bella. The paranormal family comes face-to-face with the demoness Succubus. As they battle a demoness, they all know they must find the immortality serum to not only save Tara Bella but themselves.

BOOK EIGHT:

Woman In The Mirror: Vows From The Beyond

Buried in a sarcophagus within a pyramid in Giza, Kees van Vrederic awakens and travels through the Sahara Desert of Egypt, through the Stonehenge in the United Kingdom, to his hometown Naarden in the Netherlands to unite with his beloved Marinda. With support and help from his Kasteel Vrederic family members, he searches for his buried wife Marinda. This diary is written and recited through his nephew Dr. Jacobus Vrederic van Phillip, who with the help and support of his family members, once again tries to unite the lost and buried lovers. Succubus returns with her curses but faces her worst nightmare she herself had created. In this diary, the Kasteel Vrederic family proves to the demoness her demonic powers are nothing compared to the powers and harmony of a loving family's vows from the beyond to be with one another through life or in death.

-Ann Marie Ruby

ABOUT THE AUTHOR

"Meet Ann Marie Ruby from California.
This is her story."

Ann Marie Ruby was born into a diplomatic family for which she had the privilege of traveling the world. This upbringing made the whole world her one family. She never saw a country as a foreign country yet as a neighbor who was there for her as she would be there for them. After all, isn't that what families do for one another?

Ann Marie became an author as she started to place her chosen words into the pages of her diaries. She knew she must collect all her thoughts and produce them into different diaries. Each diary became her different books.

Ann Marie's life goal is not to just write something but only what she believes in. So all her thoughts and words remained within the pages of her diaries until she realized it was time she must share them with you. Otherwise, she felt selfish and knew that was not her characteristic as she lives for everyone, not just for herself.

INTERNATIONAL #1 BESTSELLING AUTHOR:

Ann Marie became an international number-one bestselling author of twenty-six books. Alongside being a full-time author. She loves to write articles on her website where she can have a better connection with all of you. Ann Marie, a dream psychic, became a blogger and a humanitarian only because she believes in you and herself as a complete, honest, and open family.

PERSONAL:

Ann Marie is an American who grew up in Brisbane, Australia. She resided in the Washington, D.C. area, later settled in Seattle, Washington, and currently lives in California. In her spare time when she is not writing books, she loves to meditate, pray, listen to music, cook, and write blog posts.

BESTSELLING:

Ann Marie's books have placed her on top 100 bestselling charts in various countries including the Netherlands, United States, United Kingdom, Canada, and Germany. In 2020, she became a household name as her books began to consistently rank #1 on multiple bestselling charts. *The Netherlands: Land Of My Dreams* and *Everblooming: Through The Twelve Provinces Of The Netherlands*, both became overnight number-one bestsellers in the United States.

In 2020, *The Netherlands: Land Of My Dreams* also became a bestseller in the Netherlands and Canada, consistently becoming #1 on various lists and one of the top selling books on Amazon NL. *Everblooming: Through The Twelve Provinces Of The Netherlands* became #37 on the Netherlands top 100 bestselling Amazon books chart which includes all books from all genres. Ann Marie's other books have also made various top 100 bestselling lists and received multiple accolades including *Eternal Truth: The Tunnel Of Light* which was named as one of eight thought-provoking books by women.

ROMANCE FICTION:

Ann Marie's *Kasteel Vrederic* series was written in a diary fashion. She has always kept a diary herself, so she thought her characters too could keep a diary. All of their diaries became individual books yet collectively, they are a part of a family, the Kasteel Vrederic family.

OTHER BOOKS:

All of Ann Marie's nonfiction and fiction books are available globally. You can take a look at short descriptions about the books at the end of this book.

THE NETHERLANDS:

Ann Marie revealed why many of her books revolve around the Netherlands, sharing that as a dream psychic, she had seen the historical past of a country in her dreams and was later able to place a name to the country. This is described in detail in *Spiritual Lighthouse: The Dream Diaries Of Ann Marie Ruby* and *The Netherlands: Land Of My Dreams* where she also wrote about her plans to eventually move to the Netherlands.

Ann Marie has received letters on behalf of His Majesty King Willem-Alexander and Her Majesty Queen Máxima of the Netherlands after they received her books *The Netherlands: Land Of My Dreams* and *Everblooming: Through The Twelve Provinces Of The Netherlands*. Additionally, Ann Marie has received letters on behalf of His Excellency Mark Rutte, the Prime Minister of the Netherlands for her books.

WRITING:

Ann Marie also is acclaimed globally as one of the top voices in the spiritual space, however, she is recognized for her writing abilities published across many genres namely spirituality, lifestyle, inspirational quotations, poetry, fiction, romance, history, travel, social awareness, and more. Her writing style is hailed by critics and readers alike as making readers feel as though they have made a friend.

FOLLOW THE AUTHOR:

Now as you have found her book, why don't you and Ann Marie become friends? Join her and become a part of her global family. Ann Marie shall always give you books which you will read and then find yourself as a part of her book family.

For more information about Ann Marie Ruby, any one of her books, or to read her blog posts and articles, subscribe to her website, www.annmarieruby.com.

Follow Ann Marie Ruby on Twitter, Facebook, Instagram, Threads, and Pinterest:

@TheAnnMarieRuby

BOOKS BY THE AUTHOR

INSPIRATIONAL QUOTATIONS SERIES:

This series includes four books of original quotations and one omnibus edition.

Spiritual Travelers:
Life's Journey From The Past
To The Present
For The Future

Spiritual
Messages:
From A Bottle

Spiritual Journey:
Life's Eternal Blessings

Spiritual
Inspirations:
Sacred Words
Of Wisdom

Omnibus edition contains all four books of original quotations.

Spiritual Ark:
The Enchanted Journey Of Timeless
Quotations

SPIRITUAL SONGS COLLECTION:

This series includes three original spiritual prayer books.

SPIRITUAL SONGS: LETTERS FROM MY CHEST

When there was no hope, I found hope within these sacred words of prayers, I but call songs. Within this book, I have for you, 100 very sacred prayers.

SPIRITUAL SONGS II: BLESSINGS FROM A SACRED SOUL

Prayers are but the sacred doors to an individual's enlightenment. This book has 123 prayers for all humans with humanity.

SPIRITUAL SONGS III: THE RISING LOTUS

Unitedly let us rise out of the murky waters of Earth with hands held up toward the Heavenly skies, as we build a bridge of union between all the creation and the Creator through 41 prayers.

SPIRITUAL LIGHTHOUSE: THE DREAM DIARIES OF ANN MARIE RUBY

Do you believe in dreams? For within each individual dream, there is a hidden message and a miracle interlinked. Learn the spiritual, scientific, religious, and philosophical aspects of dreams. Walk with me as you travel through forty nights, through the pages of my book.

THE WORLD HATE CRISIS: THROUGH THE EYES OF A DREAM PSYCHIC

Humans have walked into an age where humanity now is being questioned as hate crimes have reached a catastrophic amount. Let us in union stop this crisis. Pick up my book and see if you too could join me in this fight.

ETERNAL TRUTH: THE TUNNEL OF LIGHT

Within this book, travel with me through the doors of birth, death, reincarnation, true soulmates and twin flames, dreams, miracles, and the end of time.

THE NETHERLANDS: LAND OF MY DREAMS

Oh the sacred travelers, be like the mystical river and journey through this blessed land through my book. Be the flying bird of wisdom and learn about a land I call, Heaven on Earth.

EVERBLOOMING: THROUGH THE TWELVE PROVINCES OF THE NETHERLANDS

Original poetry and hand-picked tales are bound together in this keepsake book. Come travel with me as I take you through the lives of the Dutch past.

LOVE LETTERS: THE TIMELESS TREASURE

Fifty original timeless treasured love poems are presented with individual illustrations describing each poem.

MELODIES OF HUMANITY: THE GOLDEN KEYS

Thirty-two poems retell the melodies of humanity, calling all humans to awaken their humanity through love, the golden keys everyone carries within their inner souls.

KASTEEL VREDERIC SERIES:

ETERNALLY BELOVED: I SHALL NEVER LET YOU GO

Travel time to the sixteenth century where Jacobus van Vrederic, a beloved lover and father, surmounts time and tide to find the vanished love of his life. On his pursuit, Jacobus discovers secrets that will alter his life evermore. He travels through the Eighty Years' War-ravaged country, the Netherlands as he takes the vow, even if separated by a breath, "Eternally beloved, I shall never let you go."

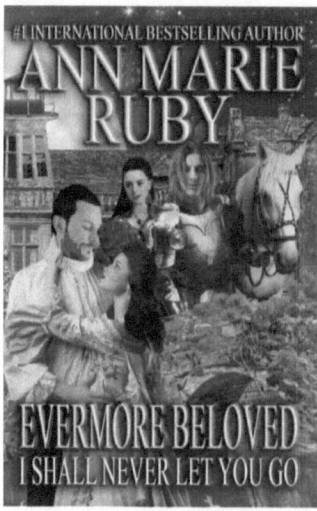

EVERMORE BELOVED: I SHALL NEVER LET YOU GO

Jacobus van Vrederic returns with the devoted spirits of Kasteel Vrederic. A knight and a seer also join him on a quest to find his lost evermore beloved. They journey through a war-ravaged country, the Netherlands, to stop another war which was brewing silently in his land, called the witch hunts. Time was his enemy as he must defeat time and tide to find his evermore beloved wife alive.

BE MY DESTINY: VOWS FROM THE BEYOND

Fighting their biggest enemy destiny, twin flames Erasmus van Phillip and Anadhi Newhouse are reborn over and over again only to lose the battle to destiny. Find out if through the helping hands of sacred spirits of the sixteenth century, these eternal twin flames are finally able to unite in the twenty-first century, as they say, "Reincarnation is a blessing if only you are mine."

HEART BEATS YOUR NAME: VOWS FROM THE BEYOND

While one is sleepless, the other twin flame is sleeping eternally. Now how does Antonius van Phillip awaken his twin flame Katelijne Snaaijer from beyond Earth, and solve a murder mystery, she is the only witness to yet also a victim of? Find out how the musical sound of heartbeats guide him to his sleeping beloved while he solves the mystery sleepless.

ENTRANCED BELOVED: I SHALL NEVER LET YOU GO

The pages of Margriete "Rietje" Jacobus Peters's love story from her diary slowly go missing from the library of Kasteel Vrederic. The twenty-first-century descendants fighting death and time must travel back in time to save their ancestors and their beloved Kasteel Vrederic. Traveling through the tunnel of light, the family of the twenty-first century must save the seventeenth-century twin flames. Rietje and her beloved twin flame Sir Alexander van der Bijl must create another paranormal, magical, historical, romantic diary for the dynasty to even exist.

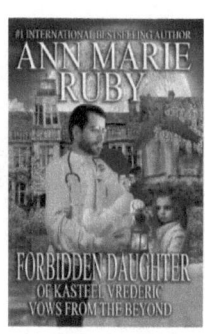

FORBIDDEN DAUGHTER OF KASTEEL VREDERIC: VOWS FROM THE BEYOND

Jacobus Vrederic van Phillip stopped pouring tears and burning himself with memories of passion to become a stone, so he could live with memories and not recreate new ones. The Vrederic family members realize the curse of past life's karma will come and meet them in this life and erase the only child who kept the dynasty going, the child known to all as the forbidden daughter of Kasteel Vrederic. The man who has sacrificed his life for all members of his family and society now must find a way to awaken his sleeping soul, recognize his twin flame, and bring back as the beloved daughter the only child he had rejected. To this world she was known as the forbidden daughter of Kasteel Vrederic.

THE IMMORTALITY SERUM: VOWS FROM THE BEYOND

Andries van Phillip, the famous pianist, gets calls from his dead twin flame Tara Bella in his dreams. All dressed in red, she roams around a burning castle trying to rescue all the people from within, without realizing she was the victim, not Andries. Now the paranormal family travels across the ocean as they fight Succubus the demoness, rescue the woman in red, and solve a murder mystery, all while they know before time ends, they must find the immortality serum.

WOMAN IN THE MIRROR: VOWS FROM THE BEYOND

An undying love story began in the sixteenth century, yet the evil eyes of Succubus wiped away the story of Kees and Marinda van Vrederic before it even had a chance. Voyage to Kasteel Vrederic where the paranormal family helps rewrite the unresolved love story of Kees and Marinda, even after their death. They must unravel the mystery behind the identity of the woman in the mirror, whom everyone seeks, before it is too late.

BRIDE OF THE IMMORTAL: VOWS FROM THE BEYOND

The ninth book in this series is coming soon.

SHATTERED WINGS: DIARY OF A CHILD BRIDE

Ahana Roy fought this unkind world to make room for her in this society, where she would not go to bed hungry. She was brought to the city of dreams where her dreams were shattered as she became a child bride. How will she fight the war of being a child bride in a city that has no idea of her existence? In her shattered dreams, she found a ghost sailor who promised to be with her, dead or alive. Following the advice of a dead sailor, Ahana wandered the streets of New York City looking for help. There she found the paranormal family of Kasteel Vrederic as her helping hands. This is the diary of child bride who said, "I had no chance in life as I was born with shattered wings."

THE BRIDE, THE GROOM, AND THE GHOST

Viviana Stella Vivour was separated from her beloved groom during the 1866 massacre in New Orleans, Louisiana. For over a century, she has been roaming the streets of "The Big Easy" as a ghost bride. Now in the twenty-first century, Viviana's spirit is transported to her reincarnated past-life groom Silas Coleridge Vivour's historic Victorian home by the Mississippi River. She is shattered to witness him facing forced retirement through ageism. Separated by a breath, Viviana and Silas come face-to-face with their past-life enemy who became a demon to separate them again. The twin flames find solace in ways they never expected as there appears Aurelius van Phillip, a mysterious young man, who can see Viviana and the demon.

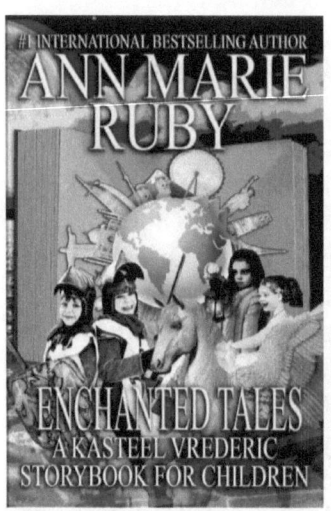

ENCHANTED TALES: A KASTEEL VREDERIC STORYBOOK FOR CHILDREN

Travel around the world in seven nights. Through enchanted tales you will meet and assist superheroes from the seven continents of this world. While there, you will learn about different cultures and landmarks. Keep your magical lanterns glowing as you help the girl with the lantern solve mysteries around the globe.

Coming Soon

BROTHER BEAR AND THE FOUR INVESTIGATORS: A KASTEEL VREDERIC STORYBOOK FOR CHILDREN

BROTHER BEAR AND THE FOUR INVESTIGATORS: A KASTEEL VREDERIC STORYBOOK FOR CHILDREN

Kasteel Vrederic's second storybook is coming soon.

www.ingramcontent.com/pod-product-compliance
Lightning Source LLC
Chambersburg PA
CBHW050551260626
47157CB00002B/521